Hunting is often a family tradition but not everyone has a family with a history of being hunters. Hunting is not actually about killing, although a real hunter will kill a deer for food, not just for sport! Disney's Bambi movie was made as anti-hunter propaganda but did little to deter this practice.

This fictional story reveals some facts about deer hunting and life in a small town. The main character, Rex Callahan is searching for property where his family can go hunting and also build a cabin for his family to use for family time together. The property they purchase provides both of these goals but the relationships with their neighbors prove to be quite complicated.

The events described concerning the hunt are real, as they are based on real-life experiences. The stories about the neighbors are fictional and not based on any real persons, living or dead.

Chapter 1

Rex was a successful real estate broker, who was searching for some land to purchase as a hunting area. Located about an hour from his residence was a farm with 600 acres and easy access from the highway. The owner was a motivated seller and Rex was definitely interested but needed to visit the property in order to make a decision.

He got his brother, Ronnie and two sons, Jack and Ernie to commit to making a visit to the farm to and check out the possibility of this being the right place. They each drove to the local Waffle House for breakfast and to discuss what this property needed to offer, if they were going to invest in it.

Ernie stressed the importance of having a place to stay when everyone gathered to go hunting or just to have a get-away location for family gatherings. If there was a house or cabin, that would definitely be a plus, even if it required some fixin' up. Jack stressed the importance of it being close enough to where everyone lived, since it would be a great rendezvous as long as it didn't take "forever" to get there. Rex, of course, brought up the selling price and what the annual taxes would be. He also questioned if there were any deer, turkeys and small game there.

Following a typical hunter's breakfast, which included eggs, a waffle, grits, toast and coffee, Rex picked up the tab for everyone, just like he always had to do! Everyone had driven to the restaurant but left their cars in the back of the parking lot, so they could go in one vehicle to the farm. It was a talkative trip, and so the half an hour drive passed quite quickly.

Turning off the main highway, there was a paved road leading into the country, which was sparsely populated with homes. On the left was the Oak Hill cemetery, easily identified by the name plate with its name boldly posted on the archway leading into it. Quite a history is associated with it, since there were civil war casualties buried there. Although they might have faced each other on the battle field, some wearing

Union Blue and others dressed in Confederate Gray; their bodies now lay silently together in the confines of the cemetery property. The longtime residents through the years, seldom brought up the history of their families or the part their ancestors played in the bloody war between the States. They would only acknowledge it was neighbor against neighbor and kin folk against kin folk at times. Additionally, veterans of various wars have had their remains honorably placed there.

The guys all agreed to stop there sometime if they purchased the farm. It would be quite interesting to check out the hallowed grounds and read the names on the headstones. You never know who might have come to this final resting spot. It could have been a renown general or an unknown private who put their life on the line, to fight for what they held dear. Besides, there might be a long-lost relative there, that no one ever mentioned. The names would give a good basis for some genealogy research.

According to the directions Rex had been given, they came to a two-track road where they turned onto a road which led them along a twisting creek. Hopefully, they wouldn't meet another vehicle coming the opposite direction because passing would certainly be challenging. There were a few spots which were wide enough for two vehicles to pass but it required some caution, or otherwise one of the vehicles would be in a ditch or go careening down the hill into the water-filled creek. Fortunately, there was no traffic that morning.

About two miles up the gravel road, there was a turn off to the property they had made the trip to scout out. The lane leading to the property was blocked by a gate but the owner, Mr. Moore was there, waiting and opened the gate so they could enter the property.

The tree canopied lane was picturesque, offering a serene drive away from civilization and into the tranquil country side. Not far from the gate was a low cement bridge, which had no sides and spanned a rushing creek.   There is nothing like the sound of running water, out in the middle of nowhere and these waters flowed over the rocks offering a soothing song. Going, further they came to a wide field which had at one time been a garden or a planted field or maybe where the old home stead once sat.   It would be the perfect place to erect a cabin, if they purchased the land.

The vehicles came to a stop and everyone got out, they stretched their legs and began to talk about what they initially saw. To the left was a ridge which stretched about 150 feet up and to the right was a ridge which was much higher, probably reaching some 300 feet into the blue skies. The field in which they stood, stretched into the valley but came to an abrupt halt about 200 yards from where they stood. It was as if the woods sprang up to block anyone or any kind of motorized vehicle from proceeding any further. A footpath could be seen leading into the trees and to whatever lay beyond. Scouting out the land was going to be a key element in the decision to buy or to keep looking. The owner, Larry informed them all of the property was clearly marked with yellow paint on the trees, showing the boundaries to this particular piece of property.

The group split up with Ernie going up the hill on the left to find the painted trees and proceed toward the rear of the property. Jack chose to go up the ridge on the right and make his way to the property line and then go towards the back of the property.   Rex continued to talk with Larry about the taxes and who used to live there. It seems Larry's great, great grandfather had owned the property but after he passed, the family just held onto the land and no one ever lived there or had any use for it. It had finally come down to Larry doing something with it, and he was happy to sell it and get the money. Ronnie quietly stood by listening.

Rex, finished talking and got the instructions about locking the gate when they left. Then he and Ronnie turned their attention to the valley and began their adventure into the awaiting wilderness. They carefully followed the footpath toward the back of the property, stepping over logs, avoiding holes filled with water and cutting briar bushes so they could move forward all with the hopes of meeting up with Ernie and Jack.

Making their way through the overgrown trail was far from easy but about an hour after leaving the vehicle, they finally got within sight of the other explorers. Ernie and Jack carefully descended the hills and made their way down to meet Rex and Ronnie, who were waiting in the valley. All was quiet except for the sound of boots slipping and sliding down the steep hillsides and an occasional caw from a crow that flew silently through the trees.

After catching their breath and drinking some water, the four followed the footpath back through the overgrown valley, arriving at the parked car. Larry had long since left but trusted Rex to secure the gate with the lock and chain which hung on the gate, as they exited the long-forgotten parcel of land which once thrived with a house and family. This would be the routine of locking and unlocking the chained gate every time they entered and exited the property, if they purchased it. The gate, though somewhat of an inconvenience, kept unwanted individuals out and would provide security for the cabin and the items which would be kept there.

The conversations about the ridges and what they found was animated as each tended to talk over the others. Before getting in the car, they took turns describing the area they had walked and what they actually saw. They agreed the woods were primarily hardwoods but there were some scrub trees. The ascending ridges had a number of flats on the sides, which could prove excellent vantage points to see any wildlife which was moving along them. Some old tree stands were noticed, which had been built in the past, but the years had made them unsafe for usage. They did identify the area as a potential excellent hunting spot. Some well-worn game trails could be spotted by the trained eye of an experienced hunter, and it looked as if there were some critters in the area. It was too early for signs like fresh rubs on the trees or scrapes on the ground but some old rubs were noticeable on the smaller trees, which meant there had been some bucks around.

Several watering holes and a manmade pond was discovered on the ridge to the right. An old trail had been made when the pond was dug but it had become impassable due to fallen trees and the undergrowth having taken over. With some hard work, the trail would become an easy access to the pond and from there, it was an easy walk up to the top of the ridge. There were deer and turkey tracks in the soft mud around the pond.

The valley had a creek which meandered its way from an underground spring in the back of the property to the front. As it neared the front, the creek bed made a sharp left turn dissecting the land into two separate areas but the cement bridge allowed for an easy passage from one side to the other. Back in the valley, there were some areas which were wide enough, if cleared out, to allow small fields for planting food for the wildlife. Also, feeders could be put out to help draw in the deer and turkeys and provide food during the harsh winters when food would be sparse in the woods.

As they prepared to leave, it was easy to picture a cabin being constructed in the field and if some of the trees were select cut, roads into the valley and up the ridges would make traversing the landscape so much easier. A tree service could provide these lanes in order for them to remove the trees they cut. Some of the trees would also provide the materials needed to construct their hunting cabin and storage buildings. It would be a win-win situation. The key would be the selling price and then the cost of building the cabin, the outbuilding, drilling a well, putting in a septic system and having electric brought to the site of the cabin and outbuilding.

As they drove out the lane, this place seemed like the answer to what they wanted and so a lively discussion ensured as they made their half-an-hour drive back to pick up their vehicles and head home. There were definitely signs of potential game there and the land was somewhat isolated but there were some other farms which adjoined on all two sides. After some discussion, it was decided Rex should meet the potential neighbors and see what they were like and if the intended usage of the property for hunting and family gatherings would be acceptable to these unknown folks.

If the ride up seemed quick, the ride home seemed like but a flashing moment, as each shared what they'd seen and actually thought about the place. It would be great, even if there was a lot to do to get it into the hideaway they envisioned. Only time would tell.

Chapter 2

A trip back to the country was in order, so Rex went alone with the intention of meeting the neighbors. The gravel lane went past the locked gate and about a half a mile further there was a driveway turning off to the right. Sitting back from the lane about a quarter of a mile, at the base of the hill was a farm house which looked freshly painted and the yard newly mowed. Behind the house was an outbuilding and sitting under the roof was a pickup truck. On the outside a tractor sat silently looking as if it had been forgotten for quite some time. The tires were flat and rust had begun to invade the exposed motor and the top of the motor housing. The seat was tipped forward but time had taken its toll, as the leather covering was gone and only the metal frame remained.

Proceeding slowly down the drive Rex scanned the front of the house and notice a man sitting in a rocking chair on the porch, which spanned the front of the house. The elderly man lifted his head to see the approaching car but didn't get up. When Rex got close enough, he put down the window and identified himself. He then asked the man on the porch, "*Do you mind if I get out and come up on the porch to talk with you? I'm thinking of purchasing the Moore farm, on the*

other side of the ridge." About that time, a large dog came around the side of the house, barking loudly and showing some large canine teeth. The man on the porch, called to the dog, "*Killer! Stop barking and come here!*" The dog immediately responded, stopped barking and ran up the steps to lay at his master's feet.

The seated man said, "*Sure, come on over, he won't bother you.*" As Rex exited the car, the dog didn't budge, even when Rex reached the stairs. "*Sit down, I'm Jeremiah Jones and this is Killer. This farm has been in my family since the 1800's. My great-granddaddy fought in the war between the States and is buried in the cemetery down the road. He survived*

16

the war but old age finally caught up to him. This was his farm and then my Pa got it and left it to me. Our kids don't have much interest in it, they moved away quite a few years ago. Just Ma and me here, along with ole faithful Killer."

Rex began by telling him who he was and what they wanted to do with the farm next door. *"I'm a real estate broker from Rivertown but am looking for some land where we can hunt and build a cabin as a get-away for our families. I have two sons, Jack and Ernie and we all enjoy hunting. The land looks like it could be a great place for both of these activities. It is important to know that you wouldn't mind us being there, hunting during the legal seasons and having a cabin where we can gather for family occasions like birthdays, holidays and as a place to enjoy some peace and quiet."*

Jeremiah nodded his head, as though he was listening and might agree. He then said, *"We used to hunt but the deer population was really diminished by the blue tongue disease back a few years ago, and the herd just hasn't recovered. There are turkeys all over the woods but we don't hunt them, just feed 'em. If you all want to hunt, its ok but we don't want anyone hunting on our property. The line between the properties is clearly marked and so, we would expect you to honor that property line. Is that understood? If not, there will be problems and we don't need that. I doubt you would want that either!"*

Rex said he understood and that would not be an issue. *"Well,"* said the old man, *"Maybe we'll be neighbors."* Rex responded, *"I hope so. By the way if there is ever any thing we can do to help you, please let us know and we'll be more than happy to assist you. My boys are really skilled workers and one of my daughters-in-law is a nurse."* After a few moments of awkward silence, Rex spoke up, *"Well, I've taken up enough of your time, so let me get out of here and I look forward to some future talks."* Jeremiah nodded his head in approval.

As Rex got up, the dog lifted his head and started to growl but Jeremiah said his name and the dog's head went back down and the growling stopped. Jeremiah did have something more to add. *"If you go on down the drive about a hundred yards further, there is a lane that goes back to the Black's farm. They are anti-hunters, so you might not get a welcome from them, just saying...."*

"Thanks," said Rex as he descended the stairs and walked across the grass to his truck. As he got in, he waved at Jeremiah and then turned around to go see the neighbors.

The lane leading to the farm was pretty grown up and was rather uninviting, especially in light of what Mr. Jones had said. The weeds rubbed against the side of the car and pot holes made the trip back to the house, which had not seen paint in many years, quite slow and difficult. When he finally got close, there were several men sitting outside around a big black pot, which had a small fire beneath it. One of the men reached for something which turned out to be a rifle. There were no smiles on the faces of any of them and Rex quickly concluded maybe this was a bad idea.

The house looked like it could use a little tender loving care but that probably wasn't going to happen. To the left of the house sat several old vehicles which were rusting away. A couple of riding mowers and push mowers were also hiding in the tall grass. There was an out building which looked like it could collapse any minute, especially if a strong gust of wind hit it just right. An old hound dog was chained to the out building where it could find shelter in winter or from the rain. There was no barking but the dog moved from side to side, as far as the chain would allow, stirring up dust from the grassless area where it was confined. The dog looked at the strange vehicle which stopped but remained silent and just stared.

The man with the rifle, which now was laying across his lap, called out, "*What do you want stranger? You ain't been 'round here before, have you?*" Rex, put down the passenger window and said he was looking for the Black family. The gun-toting man got up and walked toward the truck. His steely eyes scanned Rex and the truck and as he got close, he spit some tobacco juice onto the ground. "*Whatcha doing up here, anyway?*"He gruffly asked.

Rex, began to nervously talk to him, "*I'm Rex Callahan, from Rivertown. I'm a real estate broker and our family is thinking of purchasing the Moore farm. We are looking for land to build a cabin and have a place to go hunting during deer and turkey seasons. The cabin would also be a place to get out of the rat-race and enjoy some peace and quiet. So, I'm trying to meet you folks who would be neighbors to see if you are amicable to our buying the land and use it in these ways.*"

The bewhiskered-faced man, just shook his head. *"We don't like strangers hanging 'round or snooping 'round on our land!"* Rex retorted, *"Oh, I can understand but we know where the property lines are and they are clearly marked, so we would not be infringing on you. Mr. Jones told me you didn't like hunters, but I thought I needed to talk with you before we made any kind of a decision."*

Old man Black, spit on the ground again and said, *"As long as you stay over there where you belong, there won't be any issues. If you don't, there will be serious trouble. So, don't forget it!"* Rex shook his head, letting the old man know he heard and understood. *"Thanks, I'll not bother you any more today,"* Rex replied and turned his attention to leaving.

Rex, turned the car around and exited the driveway more quickly that he had driven in. Old man Black, stood motionless as he watched the truck drive away. The others sat motionless as the truck disappeared. Maybe the neighbors wouldn't be too bad, he thought; as long as property boundaries were closely watched, but he had an uneasy feeling about these folks, who seemed like they might be hiding something.

There was still another farm to visit and Rex wasn't sure what to expect at the next one. He turned down the gravel lane, which led back to the paved road and about half way between the gated property and the paved road was the third house. It was a modern brick house and a large barn behind it with a fence which contained several horses. The livestock looked well cared for and this place was certainly a much different looking scene than the other two farms. Somehow, on the previous trips, this site was overlooked, probably because they didn't think it would be related to the Moore farm property. It turns out it was.

Rex turned into the driveway and saw no one outside. Maybe they were in the house or out at the barn. There was a dog barking, and it ran up to the car, wagging its tail but still barking at the stranger inside the car. The barking must have alerted the resident because soon there was someone standing at the front door. The main door was open but the glass storm door was closed. It was a younger woman, who appeared to have been interrupted in cooking or doing the laundry or performing whatever chores were required to keep house.

Rex exited the car, speaking to the individual standing at the door, and said, "*My name is Rex Callahan, I'm a real estate broker who is considering purchasing the Moore farm. Our family is looking for land where we could build a cabin as a get-away and have some land on which to hunt. I am checking with the surrounding neighbors to hear what they think about our possible purchase. Mr. Jones and Mr. Black didn't oppose our plans but made clear we needed to not get onto their properties. Since you are our neighbors, on this side of the high ridge, I wanted to talk with you.*"

The lady who stood in the door said her husband was at work, so Rex would need to come back when Stan was home and they could talk. She said her name was Marsha and they had four children, all in school. *"Stan gets home about 5:30 and is off on the weekends. He's a big hunter and likes it that no one is out in the woods killing the deer and turkeys. He's glad he can take the boys and not worry about someone that he doesn't know being out there shooting at anything that moves!"*

She asked Rex for his phone number, and said Stan would call and they could settle it on the phone or Rex could come back to talk with him when he was home. She seemed quite pleasant and smiled as he turned to walk away. Rex, thanked her and backed out onto the gravel lane and headed toward home. It had been a profitable afternoon and talking to Stan would help to settle the issue. A phone call from Stan that evening was quite enlightening, because the pasture lands and hillside didn't belong to Stan but to Stan's father-in-law. That meant he had free access to the land and didn't seem to have a problem with Rex and his family owning the Moore farm. It was clear from the beginning there would be no problems about retrieving game which was shot on their property and ran onto the neighbor's adjoining property. A phone call would be appropriate to alert everyone about what was going on.

That seemed to be the final piece of the puzzle and buying the farm would be a great investment. After all, they aren't making more land, so it is always a good investment. He called his sons and related what he'd learned on the trip back to the farm and they shared in his excitement about making the land their own.

Chapter 3

The closing went smoothly and the keys to the lock were turned over to Rex and it seemed as if everything was set to change the Moore farm of old into the new Callahan farm. The negotiated price was fair and there was excitement in the air about what was going to take place in the next few months. It would be a family-affair task but the end result would be something quite long-lasting. Not only would the adults get to take advantage of the hunting lands but the land would be enjoyed by the grandkids and great-grandkids for years to come.

Rex set up Saturday as the first official work day at the new property. Everyone was called and agreed to be there by 9 am and lay out foundation for the cabin and outbuilding. Rex had the keys copied so everyone could have one, in order to have free access whenever needed. Handing them out was the first thing done when everyone was there.

Laying out the cabin location was the next order of the day, so tape measures and stakes were soon combined to establish the exact place for it to be built. It would have plenty of room for everyone and include a modern kitchen, a bath and a half, two bedrooms downstairs and a loft which could sleep six to eight. A laundry room would be located close to the downstairs bath and there would be a full basement, half of which could be finished to have another bedroom and half bath, in the future. The unfinished half would provide storage for hunting equipment, tree stands and lots of space to hang hunting clothes and camo. Boot racks could keep the muddy boots from tracking in mud to the upstairs because everyone could come in from outside down below and change out of the outer hunting clothes and come upstairs in clean clothes and shoes or socks appropriate for wearing in the house.

This would require a basement being dug and block walls erected to support the upper walls of the house. The outbuilding would be far enough away to house 4-wheelers, tractors and accompanying equipment like a bushhog, backhoe, posthole drill and even a plow. That way, these items would not be sitting out in the weather. There would also be storage for bags of corn, seeds which could be planted in the spring and a lawn mower which would be used to cut the grass around the cabin. A pulley system was put in place which would be suspended from the rafters and this provided an enclosed area where deer could be processed. After the deer was skinned, the meat could be removed from the bones and put into the freezer and then in ice chests to be taken home. The skeletons would be taken out into the woods and left so the scavengers could feast on what remained. It wouldn't be much but there would be enough for a fiercely fought-over meal for the crows and vultures.

Arrangements were made for Ajax Construction; a reputable company Rex knew and trusted, to schedule the basement being dug and lay the block walls. Since the field sloped downward toward the creek, it would be easy to have access to the basement. A double door was planned as an entrance to the basement and meant some of the mechanical equipment or 4-wheelers could be pulled in if needed.

At the same time, one of the local tree companies signed an agreement to select cut along both of the ridges. They would cut trails along the sides of the ridges and open the old trail which went to the pond. Some of the trees would be sent to the sawmill to be turned into rough cut lumber which would serve as the framing materials for the cabin. The revenue from the select cutting would also provide some funds toward the construction costs of the cabin. It was going to be a couple of months before these projects were completed, but there was a growing anticipation on getting the cement floor poured in the basement, the raising of the walls and getting the roof on the structure. Ajax would install the trusses and put on the roofing materials, which would be metal sheeting. If you've ever been in a structure with a metal roof during a rain storm, you know the unmistakable sound of the rain drops hitting the sheeting. It will definitely put you to sleep.

Since Rex had experience in building houses, he arranged for all of the necessary materials to be delivered to the property as needed. The planning went quite smoothly, except for the weather which seemed to have its own plans and that was to delay any digging which might cave in due to the wet ground. Patience won out and finally the basement was dug, the cement floor was poured and the block walls rose above the level of the ground. The walls could be nailed together and raised into place, and after being secured the trusses could be set. The heavy crane needed to lift the trusses made it over the bridge without incident and the roof and metal sheeting went on quickly. Enclosing the cabin with marine plywood and a protective sheeting was relatively easy and the only issues were sore muscles from multiple trips up and down the ladders to nail on the siding. The outside walls were finished with half logs, making it look like a log cabin!

Once enclosed, insulation had to be put in the walls before the inside was finished and the electrical and the water lines had to be run. Drilling the holes through the wooden studs was relatively easy since Rob, a brother-in-law came to head up the electrical work. He knew what needed to go where and how to run the electric lines to all the wall outlets and electric boxes in the ceilings. There was also the placing of the main breakers and a pump in the basement. It ended up being a three-day task but was made enjoyable because of the knowledge and experience Rob brought to the job site, plus he was family! The water lines were going to be Jack's job, since he was a plumber. One of the challenges was that the water would come from a well which had not yet been dug, so a line would have to be run into the basement where a pump was to be located. A hot water heater was placed in the utility room next to the upstairs full bath and close to the kitchen. The half bath on the second store also needed electric and water lines running to it. It was just a matter of knowing where things were going to be which made selecting the route much easier. Both tasks were completed, as far as was possible prior to the well being dug and the electricity being run from the road back to the cabin.

Once the well was finished, which was only 50 feet deep in order to provide good water and the electric lines were run to a pole and a transformer was installed about 25 feet from the cabin. The inside work could now be completed. With the insulation installed, the paneling went on quickly. The bathrooms were finished, as well as the kitchen. When the water was hooked up there were no leaks and the electricity didn't short circuit either. Furnishings had to be acquired and brought to the cabin. A few mistakes took place but were easily fixed and everyone's excitement grew as the spring turned to summer and fall was only a few months away. A covered porch was added all the way across the front of the cabin and was the perfect spot for an old-fashioned swing. Sitting in the swing, you could look up the valley towards the woods and see both ridges which rose from the valley floor. The trees were covered with leaves and so the field of vision was limited but in a few months the leaves would turn and drop off and you could see a long way up the hillsides and back into the valley.

Furnishings were next on the agenda and one of the local furniture stores was having a going out of business sale! Bunk beds for the two downstairs bed rooms would be perfect and 6 single beds for the upstairs loft would make it easy to accommodate those who would bunk there. The half bath up in the loft provided easy access for those late-night trips to the bathroom and a perfect place to brush teeth, take care of bodily functions or shave the beard which appeared during hunting season but would disappear prior to heading home.

On the main floor there was a counter which separated the living room from the kitchen and provided a place for 5 to eat. A small folding table could be set up in the living room, if there were more for dinner. The living room had a large u-shaped couch on the right side as you entered and two recliners were strategically placed beneath two windows which were on the left side of the living room. Against the front wall, on the left was a gun rack sitting on the floor, which could hold a dozen weapons. On the wall between the front left corner and one of the windows was another gun rack which could hold 4 more. There was plenty of fire-power for hunting or if anyone came uninvited to the cabin!

The kitchen had a refrigerator, an electric stove, a dishwasher and a double sink for doing dishes. There was plenty of cabinet space, with lower cabinets and a set on each side of the window which was directly above the sink. The counter also had a nice large storage area under it, accessible from the kitchen side.

A phone was prominently placed on the counter next to the wall. The floors were hardwood but a long runner was in place so when you stepped from the porch onto it, it ran all the way to the kitchen. An area rug covered the floor in front of the u-shaped couch.

To the right of the front door was a large flat-screen television mounted on the wall and a credenza beneath which held the cd's of movies which had been purchased to watch at night. The television had no outside antenna because they were between the two ridges and cable was too expensive for just a few days a year.

What hunting cabin wouldn't have a few trophy heads hanging on it? There were two on the wall above the gun rack and another on the wall at the back of the living room, just to the right of a staircase which was in the back-left corner and led to the loft. An albino fawn had been given to Rex by a taxidermist and it laid on the floor in the right front corner. A turkey had been preserved as if in flight and was suspended on the crossbeam which spanned the living room. A stairway led to the basement, utilizing the area beneath the stair case which led up to the loft.

The outbuilding would be built on weekends, when some of the family members would show up to work. Things didn't go as quickly in building the outbuilding as the construction of the cabin but it would be needed by the time hunting season came around. It was decided on consecutive Saturdays to meet and get the walls up and the roof on but the siding would cover only part of the building, initially. It was finished in sections, between hunting events. The tractor and additional equipment fit in easily but were not entirely secured, however that would be rectified as time went along. Remember, Rome wasn't built in a day—but Rex wasn't in charge!

As fall drew near a Labor Day family gathering was planned and everyone arrived at the property ready for a day of fun and food. A couple of folding tables were set up outside and would accommodate everyone for a delicious meal. The ladies had planned the menu and each prepared their "special" dishes and brought them to share with everyone. Following the meal and partial cleanup the kids got restless and wanted to go "exploring". The older kids agreed to take them on the trails the loggers had created. They wouldn't really go that far but the smaller ones went with wide-eyes to see the yet-to-be-explored wilderness which surrounded them. Who knows what wild animals they might encounter but the older ones promised to keep them safe?

The adult hunters got out their bows and set up a target to get in some practice since bow season would begin in just a few weeks. It was the usual competition among the guys, vying for bragging rights. Some of the arrows hit the target, and a few were right in the bullseye, but others went skidding off into the grass and required some lengthy searches to retrieve them. The misses were a source of serious ribbing and became more of a remembrance than who was the supposed "winner". It seems that every deer that walked by would not be turned into dinner. If you recall, in the language of Native Americans, vegetarian means lousy hunter!

The competition was interrupted by the sound of wailing coming from the hillside. One of the little ones had fallen and scraped their knee and the blood curdling screams which were not totally warranted got the adults attention. Ernie's wife, Pat who was a nurse, walked over to the trail and stood there with her arms open to embrace the crying child as she rushed toward her and she took her in her arms and walked into the cabin. The crying softened as Pat and the little girl disappeared through the front door and into downstairs bathroom they went. Here she tenderly applied some medicine and a band aid on the wound. They emerged and the child had a big smile on her face! There were no other causalities on the initial trek into the woods but there were some tall tales being told by the smaller children, about lions and tigers which lived in the woods. The source of these tall tales originated with the older ones, of course, who had made them up!

As the day waned and twilight began to fall, a fire was ignited in a makeshift fire pit and lawn chairs were arranged around it, while the kids sat on the ground. Everyone was enjoying the evening and time with family. The ladies had been delayed in coming out because of preparing dinner, which was left-overs from lunch. After everyone had eaten, the paper products were thrown away. When they finished cleaning up the kitchen, the ladies joined the circle of adults and kids around the fire. A few stories were shared about some of the relatives and these tales brought laughter to everyone.

Little Mikey declared he would go lion hunting this fall and get the big one that lived on the mountain! There were smiles all around, especially for his parents and grandparents, when that announcement was made. It was also agreed that Rex's father would have loved this place and might have taken it up as his permanent residence if he were still living.

There were some left over sparklers which the kids lit and ran around wildly, calling out to their Dad and Mom, "*Watch!*" All eyes were on them and they twirled the sparklers as they ran and laughed. When the sparklers finally burned out, the kids were looking for more but they had used up all of them. As the fire slowly burned down to just glowing embers, the chairs were returned to the basement and everyone gathered up their belongings and loaded the cars to return home. It was a wonderful first family outing and they were looking forward to many additional ones. Most of the younger kids were asleep before reaching the main road.

Chapter 4

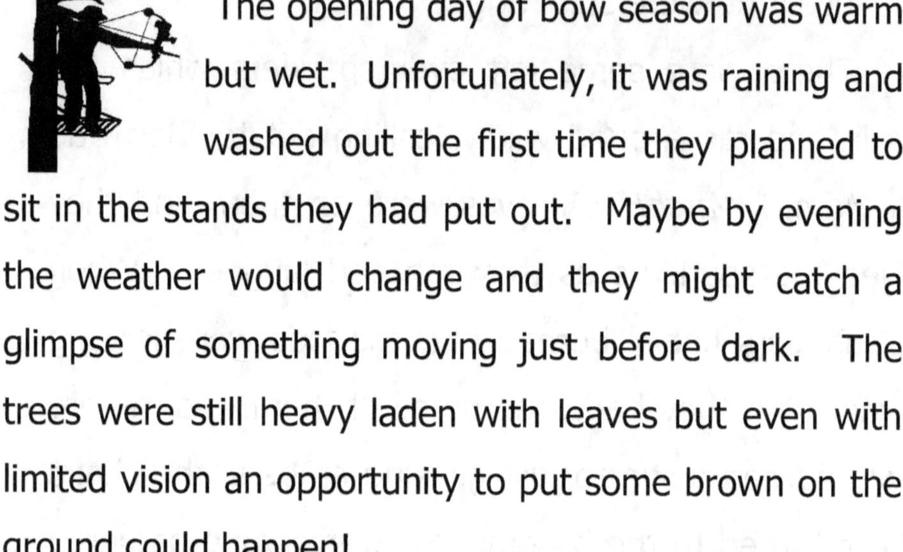

The opening day of bow season was warm but wet. Unfortunately, it was raining and washed out the first time they planned to sit in the stands they had put out. Maybe by evening the weather would change and they might catch a glimpse of something moving just before dark. The trees were still heavy laden with leaves but even with limited vision an opportunity to put some brown on the ground could happen!

About mid-morning the skies cleared and the wind picked up. Rather than just sit in the cabin, Rex decided it would be a good time to go visit with some of the neighbors. The Jones would be his first stop. So, wearing his camo he climbed into the pickup and headed down the lane to the gate. It was locked, since they had arrived on Friday evening in anticipation of getting out early for opening day. After unlocking it and exiting, he left it unlocked but put the chain on the gate without locking it. He'd be returning soon, so there was no need to have it locked.

He drove up the gravel road and turned onto the lane leading to the Jones' farm. As he got close to the house and drove in the driveway, Killer, the dog came running toward the car barking loudly. Jeremiah knew this meant someone had come to the house and he came walking around the outside and saw Rex sitting in the car. *"Come on over here, Killer won't bother you with me here."* Somewhat reluctantly, Rex exited the safety of the car and walked toward the elderly man. Killer walked alongside Rex, smelling his clothes but not making a sound.

As they rounded the corner of the house, Rex was surprised to see Jeremiah's wife sitting on a wooden chair with an apron full of green beans which she was stringing and dropping into a large bowl. She didn't stop her work as she spoke to Rex. Her face had a softness to it, like you would expect to see on a grandmother and her white hair was covered by a bonnet. Her voice was sweet sounding as she proudly announced, "*Jeremiah and I have been married 55 years and have lived on this property all of that time. We raised 3 sons, William who is a professor at a prestigious college in New York. Donald is a policeman in Los Angeles and Stanley was killed in Viet Nam and is buried in the Oak Hill cemetery.*" She continued, "*The boys don't get back much and we just don't get to see our grandchildren. Jeremiah won't fly so we are here all the time. He used to travel every week with his job. He was a salesman and became regional manager for Allis-Charmers farm equipment. He also liked to do some farming, so he was busy when home. The boys learned a lot about farm life growing up and maybe that's why they moved away and just don't come around. They call every Sunday, so at least we can keep up with what's going on in their lives and with the grandkids.*"

She then told him something which was extremely shocking. Her maiden name was Black! Yes, it was her family that lived on down the lane but how different she appeared from them.   Rex asked, "*Are those folks your family or just distant relatives?*" She smiled and utter a soft laugh. "*Yes, they are my family. Ballard is my older brother and was a teacher in the local high school, years ago. He married a woman, Carol who never seemed very friendly to the other family members and has never wanted company. After 10 years in the classroom, he seemed to change into an angry man who didn't want anything to do with the townspeople or their kids who were his students. It might have something to do with what my other brother, John Henry did. He was a pretty wild young man and one night was in a high stake's poker game. He was losing a lot of money and accused Ralph Lawrence of cheating and shot him dead. John Henry was arrested and spent 15 years in prison before being released and moved back home.   Lawrence was cheating, because they found he had an ace up his sleeve but that didn't excuse John Henry's actions.*"

"Our sister Joyce was engaged to a soldier boy who didn't come back from WWII and she just never had any interest in finding another man. She never left the farm and seems quite content to just be around family. She does come to visit Jeremiah and me once in a while. Our younger brother, Junior was always a little slow when it came to school work or catching on but he certainly made up for it by growing into a large man, who is 6 foot 8 inches and tips the scales at 350 pounds. He can be quite imposing and scary to folks who don't know him. He is a gentle giant but people tend to shun him."

"Robert, is John Henry's grandson and lives with the family. His parents were killed in a car wreck 10 years ago. He has not known any other family. He's a good boy and excellent student. So far, he's stayed out of trouble and excelled at sports. He went off to college this year."

"Why do they seem so isolated and unwelcoming to visitors," asked Rex. Betty just shrugged her shoulders and said, "*That's quite an unanswered mystery and I am not sure I know why, but I would recommend you not go around them. They don't welcome folks they don't know and I'm not always welcome, and I'm family!*"

She finished the beans and offered Rex some sweet tea, which he welcomed and thanked her for her kindness. Jeremiah had sat quietly as she talked. When she went into the kitchen for the tea, he said, "*She's a great woman. Her family is not very well liked in this community and I guess you now, know why. However, everyone knows and loves Betty. She's always been outgoing and active at church. She was certainly supportive of me, when I was gone all the time and did a great job raising our sons. I don't know why the boys don't come around but she just takes it in stride.*"

Betty returned and the sweet tea was delicious. Small talk filled in the next 15 minutes and Rex, thanked them and stood up to return to his car.

"Remember" he said, *"we are your neighbors and if there is anything, we can do to help you, please don't hesitate to call us. Here is my business card with my phone number. I have enjoyed our visit and look forward to more visits."*

Killer had been laying quietly by Jeremiah but raised his head as Rex rose from his seat on the chair. Jeremiah spoke the dog's name and he put his head back down. Rex headed to the car and drove back to the farm, planning to get out in the woods later that afternoon and see if he could spot some deer movement.

He drove past the gate and headed to the brick house to see if Stan was there. As he turned into the driveway, he saw Stan outside with his boys and was tending to the horses. Rex, stopped the car and called to them. Since they had only talked on the phone, Stan didn't recognize Rex and the boys had been in school so none of they had met face to face, prior to this.

Rex identified himself and Stan introduced his boys. The oldest was Joshua who was in high school and was really into horses. David and Ruth were twins who were middle school students and Matthew was in the 4th grade and liked to go hunting with his dad! *"Speaking of hunting,"* Rex said, *"Did you get out this morning? The rain kept us in the cabin but we're going to head out this evening."* Stan replied, *"No. Just didn't have time. Josh was supposed to have been in a parade this morning but the rain cancelled it. We did go to town and we just got home and it's time to take care of the horses.*

"So, the fields and hillsides on the other side of the road are yours?" Asked Rex. Stan looked over in that direction and said, *"Actually they belong to my father-in-law but we hunt on them and Josh likes to ride his horse in the field and on some of the trails which go up on the ridge. He won't be riding up there during hunting season, so don't worry about him or his horse scaring off the deer. It's good to know you guys*

are over there because we worried about poachers and someone mistaking the horse for a deer and shooting it or Josh." Rex reassured him, *"We don't just shoot at anything that's moving.   We always know what is clearly in our sights, before squeezing the trigger."*

Rex went on to say, *"It was nice to meet your wife the last time I was here.   She certainly seemed friendly, even to a stranger."* Stan spoke up, *"That might be because she's a PK (preacher's kid) and has never met a stranger!"* *"Well,"* Rex responded, *"The next time we have a family get together, we will have to invite you and your family so we can get better acquainted.   Our grandkids are about the same age as your kids and I'm sure they would get along great."*

Rex looked at his wrist watch and said, *"I've got to get going if I'm going to get out in the woods.   I'm sure my boys are wondering where I am."* About that time, his phone rang, it was his son calling to see where he was and when he'd be back.   *"See you around,"* Rex said and headed for the truck.   He backed up and drove back to the gate, opened it and drove through and then locked it, because they'd be there tonight and wouldn't head home until after hunting the next morning.

He entered the house, went to the refrigerator and got a bottle of water and tucked in into his backpack. He then went downstairs to get his bow, complete with an arrow quiver and arrows, put on his hunting boots and looked at the two sons who were chomping at the bit to get going. *"Ok, let's go!"* He said. So out the door they went, with Rex locking the door behind them. A key was placed under a nearby rock, so if someone came in early, they could still get in and not have to wait for the others to come back.

They didn't take a 4-wheeler because they weren't actually going that far. Each went toward their selected hunting area. Jack went to the right, Ernie went to the left and both started to climb the respective hillsides. Rex followed the trail back through the trees in the valley. The only sounds were water dripping from the leaves which were still a canopy to the woods and a crow calling as it flew high in the sky. The walk was without any loud noises, due to the early rains, except the occasion stick which snapped under their boot as they walked. Getting to their respective stands under such conditions would not scare away any deer who might be out feeding. The possibility of seeing something before dark was exhilarating. Each thought in the back of their minds, *maybe that BIG one will walk out and I'll be able to have a good clean shot and the first deer taken will be mine, and I'll have those bragging rights, forever!*

The three hours they had to sit quietly on stand, passed rather quickly. However, not only did the big one not come by, not a single deer showed up. Although Ernie said he did see what he thought was a deer, as he strained to see through the leaves on the trees but it never showed itself enough to be identified. The few minutes it hung around was exciting but non-productive. However, it would be a good conversation piece at the dinner table that night. Neither Jack or Rex saw anything, not even a squirrel. As darkness began to creep in and the temperatures dropped, they slipped down the ladder on their tree stand and headed towards the cabin. It would be completely dark before Ernie would get off the ridge and the bad part was that his flashlight was back at the cabin, a mistake you don't want to make when going through unfamiliar terrain. He did get a few branches across the face and stumbled over a few unseen logs but managed to get back without any injuries. It was a lesson learned and wouldn't be repeated!

Rex had already started to prepare supper, which was spaghetti with bread, a salad and for dessert it was cherry pie made by Vicky and brought to the cabin! It was a standing rule, whoever cooked didn't have to clean up and do the dishes. Both boys, gladly pitched in with both devouring the meal and working together to clean up the kitchen.

Conversation at supper had focused on what they had seen while on their stands that afternoon. Ernie said the leaves were problematic and whatever he saw off in the distance couldn't be identified as either a buck or doe. Jack and Rex had to admit they were "skunked" and didn't get an eye on anything. Maybe tomorrow morning would be more productive. The topic changed to remembering some of the other hunting experiences they had shared over the years, when deer were killed and proudly brought back to the hunting camp. As a matter of fact, the deer heads which adorned the cabin walls were a few of the successful hunts they had in other years and in other places. But they had grand ideas of what this property might produce since it hadn't been seriously hunted in several years. After watching an old John Wayne movie, they called it a night because 5 am would come early! The cabin was dark by 10 o'clock, except for the night light that shown in the upstairs bathroom. All three had decided to sleep in the loft and it was a restful but short night.

Chapter 5

The silence and darkness were broken by the buzzing of the alarm clock and lights came on, causing squinting of the eyes. *"I can't believe it's time to get up already" said* Jack. *"Me neither" echoed* Ernie. Both laid in their bunks but Rex, who was already downstairs and started to cook breakfast, called up to them to get up, or they would be late, especially if they didn't get down there to eat. The counter was the breakfast table and scrambled eggs, bacon and toast were on the menu. Rex put an equal amount on each plate but the boys would have to butter their own toast and put jelly on, if they wanted it. There was coffee brewing and milk in the refrigerator. They came down the stairs and sat down at the counter. *"Man, it just doesn't get any better than this,"* was Ernie's' assessment of the whole situation! *"Our own cabin, plenty of property to hunt,*

great food, getting to spend time with family and here we are!" said Jack.

Breakfast was served on paper plates and what little there was to clean up was simplified as they threw away the plates and plastic knives, forks and spoons and rinsed out the coffee cups. It didn't leave much to do when they got back. The task at hand was to get their gear together, pack a snack or two for the morning hunt and get out in the woods before daylight broke. Jack went to the front door and opened it, he turned on the porch light in order to check the temperature on the thermometer which graced the front of the cabin. "*42*" he said as he turned off the light and closed the door. This would help them know what to wear when they sat out in the woods all morning. The temperature in the 40's meant very little in the way of thermal clothes but a water-proof jacket would come in handy due to the light fog and residue of yesterday's rain.

The backpacks were filled with snacks, water and some sodas which had screw on caps, making it easy to open and close when they took an occasional drink during the hours of waiting patiently on the deer stand. There was a dry shirt, a pair of gloves, a release for the bow, some toilet paper, should the need arise and their cell phones went in one of the pockets with a zipper so it wouldn't be lost when walking in or out, all placed in their backpacks . Dressed in camo, they split up in the dark, just as they had yesterday afternoon but in the darkness, each could be followed by the light of their flashlight piercing the blackness. Their entrance was quiet, once again due to the wet ground and fortunately it wasn't muddy or slippery going up the hillsides to their stands on the ridge.

Arriving at the stand, each would slip off the tee-shirt which had become wet from sweating due to the walk in and put on the dry one. The wet one went in the bottom of the backpack and everything else was placed on top of it. It was breaking day so seeing the release and putting on a camo shirt was easy done. Now, it was up the ladder to get situated for a potentially long wait or maybe a brief wait for the ghosts of the forest as deer are known, to come slipping along. The deer would probably be feeding and heading to their bedding spots, so it would not be a deer running that they would hear, but it would be the soft sound of leaves being turned over as the deer searched for acorns to fill its stomach. Good hearing is a necessity and staying alert, especially when the leaves are still on the trees are required if one is to spot a deer!

The minutes turned to hours and nothing was seen or heard. But about 8:45, Ernie thought he heard something moving along the ground. He strained his eyes in the direction of the sound but couldn't locate the source. Then, there it was, a big grey squirrel hunting for breakfast and scampering from log to log and disturbing the leaves which covered the ground.

Oh well, a false alarm never hurts, because it will keep a hunter on his toes for the real deal, a deer!

Jack got a bit antsy while sitting on the stand and decided to stand up, to see if his view could be improved. It was a bad decision; his movement spooked a deer which had been quietly making its way along the ridge. It picked up his movement, immediately snorted and bounded down the ridge, with its tail or "flag" waving goodbye. Patience is not only a virtue; it is a basic requirement if you're going to still hunt, especially from a tree stand! His opportunity had just vanished and it would probably mean there would be no other deer coming that way. As the morning hours passed, that assessment was correct and he never saw another deer that day from his vantage point in the stand. However, it did let him know this was a very good place and with more patience, a deer might be taken at this location.

Rex had gone back to the very back of the property which adjoined a large man-made lake. The land that belonged to the Blacks was further to his left and still included some of the ridge which then dropped down onto the back portion of their farm. He had hung a stand on the back ridge which served as a saddle from the ridge on the left to the ridge of the right. On the other side of the back ridge was a sloping hillside which ended at the edge of a lake. The undergrowth was extremely thick and pine trees served as perfect bedding areas for the deer during hot days. It was also an excellent hiding spot when or if hunting pressure became too strong.

He climbed up in his stand and hadn't been there very long when he caught glimpse of a doe and two fawns making their way along the ridge, as they moved from the left ridge to the higher right one. They were out of shooting range, so he just watched them carefully in order to observe their habits. The mother led the way and the two fawns trailed along behind. With his binoculars he noted that the fawn which trailed the mother was a doe and other little one was a button buck. These two were born during the spring of this year and would stay with their mother until next spring, when she would give birth to another baby or set of twins. Twins are not uncommon for the deer and it helps to replenish the herd more quickly. After about 15 minutes of milling about, they got out of sight and he put down the binoculars and leaned back against the tree, waiting for some others to come by. His waiting would pay off.

About an hour later, he caught sight of something moving down below his stand, on the valley floor. It was a deer and sure enough there were horns, however they were not very big and didn't even extend out beyond the buck's ears. This was probably a 2-year old and not a shooter, especially this early in the hunting season. He watched as it walked rather quickly across the flat valley floor and up the right ridge, climbing it like it was flat ground. He quickly got out of sight due to the leaves, but Rex could occasionally hear him as he made his way up the hillside. Although he didn't get a shot at anything, he did at lease see 4 deer and it got his adrenaline pumping. This would be where he would commit to hunting during bow season and maybe even during gun season.

The sun reached its zenith and sunlight cascaded through the trees, exposing sights none of the hunters had previously noticed. They had planned to return to the cabin just after noon and pack up to head home, but it would give each some time to do a little more exploring of their areas. The sun had dried out the leaves and each step produced a crunching sound but the actual hunting was over for the day and doing some additional scouting was on the agenda.

Rex carefully came to where he had seen the deer cross the valley floor and took note of the trail which was easily distinguished in the fallen leaves. There were even some old rubs from years past, which were visible on the ridge as it ascended toward the top. He stepped over the trail, so as to not leave his scent in it, and walked on down toward the cabin, stopping regularly to scan the ridges on each side. There were some places where it was even too steep for a deer to climb, much less a human being, but every now and then a valley would appear and it offered the potential for access or egress. He walked over to see if any tracks were to be found but there were none. These might be where a deer would run if frightened or spooked, so it was good to know should that situation ever arise.

Jack, had gotten down and slipped along the edge of one of large flats. About half way back to the cabin, he looked down through the foliage and could see the house where Stan and his family lived. It was a long way from the flat to the bottom and once the leaves were gone, it meant if he was hunting at that spot, he was on their property and should get back up on the top of the ridge. He made his way up the ridge and there was an old tree stand, prominently built in a huge oak tree right in the intersection of the three large branches which grew out of the massive trunk. He kept that spot in mind and figured he could hang another stand, nearby and maybe it would prove productive. He made his way down the ridge toward the cabin and came to the pond, it was actually about 200 yards right below the old tree stand and would make it easy to find, even in the darkness. Jack decided to just go straight down the ridge to the cabin. He found a few trails which crossed it, crisscrossing the ridge from the front of the property to the back but nothing which really caught his eye. About half way down, he decided to venture off toward the front of the property and see what was there. About 100 yards from where he had stopped was a gentle sloping ridge which veered off the main ridge and so he followed it. It came out at the creek and had a well-worn deer trail right in the middle of it. This was a key to the pattern of how the deer probably could slip up the ridge undetected and undisturbed. Maybe a stand should be hung near the top of this small ridge, where it intersected the high ridge which made its way all the way to the back of the property and connected to a piece of the Black's property.

Ernie had not ventured away from his stand and when it was getting dark, just headed down to the cabin. The trio arrived back at different times but had some tales to tell and didn't hesitate to share what their scouting had produced. The more spots they had to hang stands from which to hunt provided a variety of options of where to go, according to the weather or other conditions, and improved their odds of finding that wall-hanger they were looking for. After hanging their hunting gear in the basement, it was time for a shower and packing up clothes and putting the suitcases in the truck.

The first couple of days of the hunt were memorable but each of them was looking forward to many more hours in the woods and at the cabin. Only time would tell what kind of success might await their efforts.

Chapter 6

Bow season passed rather quickly, without any success in harvesting a deer. The leafy canopy had been transformed from green to various shades of red, orange and yellow before turning brown and floating down to become a brown carpet on the ground. With the leaves no longer suspended on the limbs, the visibility dramatically increased.

On the opening day of gun season the alarm broken the silence in the cabin and the light pierced the darkness because it was time to rise and shine! Rex was the first one to slip on a pair of jeans and socks and gently descend the staircase to prepare breakfast for all the hunting party. He turned on the light in the kitchen and as he did, he could hear the shuffling of feet in the loft as the previously sleeping hunters got up and began to put on their thermals and socks in preparation of exiting the warm cabin and soft beds for the cold outside and the non-so-soft seats in the deer stands.

The door from the bedroom just off the kitchen opened and some family guests emerged. They were stretching and yawning, trying to wake up and get ready for the excitement of opening day of gun season in the deer woods. Patrick was a good friend of Jack and they worked together. The other male was Wayne who had gone to college with Ernie and they had remained friends through the years. Both guests were experienced hunters but had not had the opportunity to scout the property and know just where they would set up to have a good chance to be successful on this hunt. It would be Rex who would suggest where the boys might take them, with possibility of seeing see some deer on the move as daylight washed away the darkness. Jack and Ernie could lead them close to the possible place to set up to hunt and would drop them off near the suggested spot. It would be up to them to pick the actual spot to sit and wait. A camp chair would make the wait far more comfortable than sitting on the ground or if they decided to not climb one of the ladders and utilized a tree stand.

Breakfast was eaten quickly, since the decision made the night before was something quick and simple, either cereal or oatmeal and donuts. The coffee would put a little something warm in their stomachs and it was going to be needed. Jack checked the thermometer on the front porch and announced the temperature as 29 degrees! This would mean dressing warm for the early morning hours and hoping the weather forecast was accurate, since they predicted the temperatures reaching into the mid-40's by mid-afternoon.

Everyone had packed a lunch, put several bottles of water in their backpacks, along with additional thermal clothes to change into after reaching their destination. The cold air meant everyone could see their breath as they made their way up the hillsides and into the woods. There was frost on the leaves which muffled the sound of the men walking and made the hillside somewhat slippery and it required they not get in a hurry. There is nothing worse than slipping and falling while trying to ascend the steep hillsides. When you do, it results in a good amount of noise and always has the potential of injury. This could also cause the scope to be bumped and the gun would no longer be sighted in which is a major problem when hunting!

The light of the flashlights could be seen every once in a while, shining through the trees and along the hillside as each of the hunters headed in separate directions. As daylight began to break the flashlights were not needed and avoiding low branches was much easier and stepping over rocks which were hidden in the darkness were avoided which often caused someone to stumble, before they became clearly visible. It also meant that when the hunters reached their stands, they would be able to see the clothes they had planned to change into, which was in their backpack along with gloves, toboggans, binoculars, rangefinders and snacks; as well as lunch and something to drink. With daylight breaking, it meant the two newcomers had an excellent view of the surrounding area, in order for them to decide the best spot to set up for the morning hours.

Although they all left the cabin at the same time, it was Rex who reached his stand at the back of the property first, where he'd set up near the natural saddle connecting the two ridges. He hadn't been settled in for very long, possibly 35 minutes when a movement off to his left drew his full attention. He very slowly turned his head so he could see the entire ridge which stretched upward toward the top of the ridge. Slowly walking along, with his head down and feeding on the acorns which were in abundance in the leave was a big buck whose antlers were immediately visible. When the buck raised his head, the rack extended beyond the deer's ears and his brow tines appeared to be 6 inches or more in length. This was quite likely a mature deer, over 4 years old, and was definitely a shooter.

Rex kept his eyes locked on the deer and when the deer's head would disappear behind a tree, he began the task of slowly bringing his gun up to his shoulder, getting the safety off and looking through the scope to locate the enormous buck. The buck never seemed to sense Rex's presence and when the buck stepped into an open shooting lane Rex put the crosshairs right behind the shoulder and squeezed the trigger!

The buck leaped in the air and tucked his tail as it turned and bounded back up the ridge about 20 yards. Rex watched and could see the deer stagger and then go down it had been a clean kill shot and now all the real work began. Rex leaned back on his stand and could feel the coldness from the tree through his camo and hat. He took several deep breaths and then began to gather up his gear which included his backpack which was hung on a hook that he'd screwed into the tree earlier in the hunting season. This provided a secure spot to hang it and kept it out of the way but made it easily accessible when he wanted to put something in it or take something out.

Taking his time, Rex made his way down the 10 steps on the ladder and reached the ground safely. He had his backpack slung over one shoulder and his gun had been lowered down on a rope so he didn't have to carry it up or down the ladder. This practice proved quite safe and meant there was no chance of dropping the gun while climbing or banging it on the ladder stand which could damage the gun itself.

Once he reached the ground, he took off some of the thermal clothes, put back on his orange vest which is required when gun season comes along and leaving the discarded clothes and backpack at the base of the tree made his way toward the deer which lay motionless on the ground. Drawing near he carefully examined the animal which was laying on its left side. He didn't want to stand over a massive deer which wasn't actually dead, so took his rifle and touched the carcass. If it wasn't dead he could easily finish it off with another shot. However, there was no movement and now the task of field dressing began.

After opening the carcass from the back to the neck and getting all of the stomach, intestines, heart, lungs and esophagus removed, it would be much easier to drag the deer back to the cabin. The so-called gut pile was left on the ridge, which would draw the buzzards and other scavengers to clean it up. Most likely it would not be there tomorrow, if someone came walking by.

Experience had taught them to have a wheeled cart available to bring the deer back or a 4-wheeler to ride out to where the deer was down and put it on the front rack, rather than dragging it on the ground. This meant, Rex had a hike back to the cabin but he would be able to ride the 4-wheeler on the return trip. Since his route was along the valley floor, it would be quite easy. During the early months, the trail had been cleared and expanded as briars and low hanging limbs and encroaching vegetation were removed.

At 9 am, the hunters had agreed to check in with one another by text to get an update. Everyone had heard the earlier shot and now heard the roar of the 4-wheeler as it made its way back through the valley. After reaching the deer, Rex's phone vibrated not once or twice but four times, as each asked what he'd seen. His response included a picture and the news he was heading back with the dead buck. He might want to gloat but it wasn't a competition and he knew his boys would be glad their dad got the first deer. He would have been equally thrilled if one of his boys had gotten the first one.

Meanwhile, the reports were interesting but no one had been as successful as Rex. Ernie saw a doe about daylight and then about 8:30 a doe with twin fawns had come near. Jack saw a spike buck and later a 4-pointer but they weren't shooters and he simply watched them for about a half an hour until they walked down the ridge toward the pond. Patrick had not seen anything even though he was within sight of the pond, so the deer Jack saw didn't make it all the way down to the pond or had spotted him up and slipped quietly away. Wayne reported seeing 3 turkeys and a bunch of squirrels. He also spotted a fox trotting along on one of the flats which was near the top of the ridge.

When Rex got back to the cabin, he took the deer to the hoist in the outbuilding and hung it up in the shade, even though the temperatures were still in the upper 30's. It wouldn't spoil but he didn't want to waste such a nice kill. Taking the garden hose, he rinsed the insides of the hanging deer, to get as much blood out as possible and check to see if he had gotten all the viscera removed. He found a stick to place inside the cavity, between the ribs so it could cool.

During the next 4 hours, shots were heard off in the distance but none close-by. Apparently, none of the four hunters from the cabin had an opportunity to take a shot and so after the silent hours passed, three of them headed back to the cabin, only Jack remained on stand. Maybe just before dark, they could get back out there and have a better chance to see a buck and get to put brown on the ground!

Since each one had eaten the lunch they packed, before returning to the cabin, it was only a matter of having a snack while waiting for the afternoon hours to pass. The three returning hunters wanted a full report from Rex on his kill and they got it. Naturally they walked out to where the deer was hanging and admired the magnificent animal. Rex asked for a little help in skinning the deer and they readily agreed.

The skin was slit around the neck, down each of the four legs and a tennis ball was slipped under the skin at the back of the neckline. A rope was tied around it and then attached to the trailer hitch on the back of the truck. Slowly the truck began to drive away from the hanging deer and the skin was easily pulled off from the hanging animal with no damage to any of it. Thus exposed, the task at hand was to remove the various cuts of meat and put them in the ice chest which conveniently sat on the ground, just to the left of the hanging deer. The meat would then be placed in the freezer.

Rex was quite skilled at this process and by the time he finished, there was very little left hanging but the deer's skeleton. They let it down onto the 4-wheeler and took it out into the woods and left it there. What little pieces of meat left on the bones would be food for some small scavengers which would complete the task of removing all the meat from the bones. The head, complete with antlers would be put in the freezer and the skin would be rolled up and also put in the freezer. Later, when they headed home, the head could be dropped off at the taxidermist to be mounted and the skin used to complete the work on another trophy, which would be prominently displayed at the cabin.

About an hour and a half before sunset, the three headed back out hoping to see something. Jack had been on the right ridge all day but had nothing exciting to report. As the afternoon waned, the text messages flowed between the four. They alerted Jack as to their movements and took only a flashlight, bottle of water and a camo jacket with them. Their phones were always with them and had been recharged while back at the cabin. What could be worse than having no phone? Having a phone that was dead or forgetting to silence the ringer which would spook a deer when it rang!

The ebbing sunshine produce no shots but Jack did see the silhouette of a deer as the light faded. Unfortunately, he couldn't tell if it was a buck or doe. Since, they had decided to only take mature bucks this hunting season, Jack didn't take the shot. There was no regret on Jack's part because it meant there just might be a return of that deer and if it was a doe, a big buck might be trailing behind her. The rut, when does are in heat, will cause the bucks to come out of hiding and run them all over the woods! A buck chasing a doe is not thinking with the right head and it will probably cause him to lose more than his head, it will cost him his life!

Darkness closed in as the hunters put their flashlights to use and made their way back to the cabin. The lights of the cabin made it shine like a jewel in the darkness and was a welcomed sight. Inside, Rex had begun to fix dinner. Tonight's menu included chili, crackers, cheese for a topping, ice tea or sodas and a Bundt cake for dessert, graciously supplied by a daughter-in-law.

Patrick and Wayne got the privilege of washing the dishes and cleaning up the kitchen. There was nothing left of the chili but the cake would provide dessert or a snack for another time. Following the cleanup, they all gathered in the living room to watch a movie before calling it a day. Poor Jack wasn't able to stay awake for the entire movie and nodded off about half way through. The rest watched it to the end, woke Jack and then all of them headed off to prepare for bed with some taking a shower, brushing their teeth and changing into clean skivvies and t-shirt. The bed was welcomed and sleep came rather easy for the group.

Snoring could be heard coming from the bedroom downstairs due to exhaustion having overtaken the two residents. A nightlight shown softly in the downstairs bathroom as did a nightlight illuminate the upstairs, half bath. Night trips to the bathroom were safe but not very frequent by these young guys! It was another story for Rex.

It had been a good day but tomorrow could hold an equal or greater opportunity for the deer hunters but only time would tell.

Chapter 7

The next couple of days failed to produce sightings of any deer which they would shoot. Numerous does and young deer walked around but no bucks were with them or trailing them, yet. The small saplings and mid-size trees were starting to show the rubbing of the bucks as they practiced sparing and numerous scrapes began to appear on the ground under overhanging branches. The rut was beginning and it would mean the bucks will come out of hiding and not just move under the cover of darkness.

Since no deer were being seen the hunters chose not to just sit idly by and got down and slipped around hoping to peer over the top of the ridge or around a tree and see a deer feeding or walking casually along. Taking a step or two and scanning the area can be hard to do. If the hunter gets impatient, he will start moving too quickly and give his location away as he steps on crunching leaves or sticks which break beneath his boot. Even this stalking method didn't turn up anything but it would lead to some interesting discoveries.

Ernie was on the ridge to the left which was adjacent to the Jones' property toward the front part of the ridge, while the Black's property connected toward the very back of the farm. As he made his way along the top of the ridge, he kept looking to his left and scanning the areas on the other side of the property line. There is just something about the property next door that has a greater allurement than where you are and it got the best of him.

He ventured down the side of the ridge, slowly watching for any movement but there was nothing to be seen. Rather than going back toward the road, he set his sights on moving toward the rear of the property. With the leaves no longer in place, he could see all the way to the bottom of the ridge. To his surprise the lane which ran by the Jones' house and to the driveway of the Blacks didn't end at the barn behind their house. It went through a gate and ran all the way back to the base of the ridge which connected the two ridges. As he looked at it, he could tell it wasn't abandoned but appeared to have some regular and current use.

Rex had warned him about going down onto the property which belonged to the Blacks but he kept descending the hillside. He slipped down going from tree to tree to cover his movements and since he had removed his orange vest and hat and wore only his camo. He thought it made him just about invisible unless someone saw him moving. He felt he would blend in and go unnoticed especially if anyone happened to look toward the back of the property.

When he finally got down to the lane he walked on away from the house and much to his surprise he saw the opening of a cave or maybe an abandoned mine. He slipped over to have a look in but the interior was too dark to be able to make out how deep it went into the 

hillside or what might be lurking inside. It would be a perfect place for a bear, fox, coyote or even a turkey to find refuge. He turned on his flashlight and shined it into the darkness.

What he saw was quite unexpected. Shining the beam of light from side to side, it reflected off a variety of items.   There were flat screen televisions, computers, answering machines, printers, copiers, bicycles, motorcycles, scooters and buckets full of jewelry. He thought this must be the items which were reported stolen over the past months of unsolved break-ins in the city. Maybe this explained why the Blacks didn't want anyone snooping around their property!

Ernie made a hasty exit and started back up the ridge, when he heard someone yell, "*Hey, you, what are you doing here? You don't have any right to be on our property, snooping around. I'm going to get my Pa and he'll teach you not to come snooping around.*" It was Junior who called out to him and at 6 feet 8 inches in height, no hair or beard, he was quite a scary sight!

Junior turned to run toward the house and Ernie thought he had better get up the ridge and back on their property before they catch him where he didn't belong! He hurried back up the ridge, slipping and sliding every few steps but reached the top of the ridge and kept going down the other side to the valley below. He guessed he was safe and maybe nothing would come of the unexpected encounter with Junior. But he couldn't have been more wrong.

When he got back to the cabin to his surprise Rex asked him where he'd been. He wasn't going to lie so he admitted to going over the top and onto the Black's property. He began to tell him what he had seen when an old truck came to an abrupt halt outside the front of the cabin. It was old man Black and he didn't seem very happy! He barged  through the front door, took a momentary look around then began to curse and yell at Rex and Ernie, asking "*What the hell were they doing snooping around on my property?*

Rex had been standing in the kitchen fixing a couple of peanut butter sandwiches for Ernie and himself. Ernie was seated at the kitchen counter, with his back to the front door, when it flew open and Ballard marched into the room. Rex, turned abruptly and spoke over Black's rant. "*Whoa, there fella; what are you so upset about? You need to calm down, so you don't have a stroke. What's the problem that has you so upset?*" Black explained, "*One of you fellers was down on our property and Junior saw him and told him stay there while he came to get me. When we got back, no one was there but he knew it was one of you! So, who was it and just exactly was he doing?*"

Rex said, "*Yes, my son did come over the property line and was on your property. I want apologize for his intrusion! I can assure you it WON'T happen again!*" Old man Black, stood there glaring at them and finally said, "*It better not or you'll be sorry! Mark my word, no one comes snooping around and lives to tell about it!*"

Ballard turned quickly and marched back out the door not bothering to close it. He got in his truck, started it, hastily turned around and drove away. It was not a pleasant visit and Ernie was trying to be apologetic to his dad but Rex said to him, "*I warned you about going over there. They must be hiding something.*" He was interrupted by Ernie who said, "*You aren't kiddin'. I found a cave or old mine and it was full of stuff.*" Rex said, "*What kind of stuff?*" Ernie began to describe what he'd seen, "*Well, there were flat screen tv's, computers, printers, bicycles, motorcycles, scooters and buckets full of what looked like jewelry! You know, items which have been reported stolen from town according to the local newspaper. The break-ins were never solved and no leads have ever been revealed.*"

Rex's next comment might have surprised Ernie as he said, "*Maybe you're right but we can't just jump to conclusions without any proof! Do you think we can go to the police and tell them to go search back there? And, if we do, what do you think old man Black will do? His warning was certainly a threat!*" "*Yes*", responded Ernie. "*But what are we going to do?*" "*Nothing right now,*" said Rex.

Since it was still early in the afternoon, Rex and Ernie went out on the porch and sat in the swing to have their sandwich and soda. Silence prevailed as they swung back and forth, neither spoke. Suddenly the silence was broken by the sound of a nearby gunshot. It sounded like it came from the left ridge where Ernie had left Wayne. Rex and Ernie looked at each other as if to say, *What now?* Neither said it out loud, but they imagined that old man Black had retaliated and shot at something or someone. Hopefully that someone was not Wayne.

As they sat there for what seemed like an eternity, Ernie's phone rang, it was Wayne. *"Hey, man, we heard a shot from your way, are you ok?"* "Well," Wayne started, *"I am but I'm not."* *"What do you mean,"* Ernie quickly asked? Wayne continued, *"I saw a big 8-pointer and shot at him. Wasn't sure if I hit him, so I got down and walked over to where he was standing and sure enough there was blood! But he didn't go down he ran over the ridge toward one of the adjacent farms. I think you said to not go after it so I'm just standing here trying to decide what to do!"* Ernie quickly responded, *"Whatever you do, DON'T go over the ridge, old man Black was just here mad as an old wet hen because I was down there and his crazy son, Junior saw me. Come on back to the cabin and forget about the deer."*

Rex and Ernie, looked at each other and Ernie said, *"Well, that's one deer that won't be processed unless the Blacks find it and do something with it. It's a shame we can't retrieve it."* Rex didn't want to say the obvious, but he did anyway. "*Yes, if you hadn't gone down there, maybe they would have allowed us to drop over the top of the ridge and get it. Not now! And I don't think it would ever be safe to look and I'm certainly not going to ask for permission!*" Ernie, hung his head and nodded it in agreement.

Wayne came walking with his shoulders drooping and head down. He wanted to get that deer even if he didn't understand why not to go. He complied with their order to not to go looking for it. Afterall, it was their property and he was a guest so he needed to abide by whatever rules they established.

Jack had not checked in all day, nor had Patrick but that wasn't unusual. Jack and Patrick had met up about noon and sat down together watching different ways from where they sat on the ground. Their conversation was in hushed tones, so as to reveal their position. Whether it worked or not was hard to determine because they didn't see anything moving up the hillside or along the flat on the ridge. They could see Stan's house and the large field which stretched along the bottom of the hillside. The young kids were outside playing and Josh was riding his horse in the field. Stan wasn't home from work because there was only one car in the driveway.

They hadn't seen Stan or his youngest son Matt head out into the woods to do any hunting. Maybe this evening they would venture out but after Stan got home he went in the house and never came back out except to call Josh in for dinner.

Knowing the day was coming to a close Jack and Patrick decided to slip over the edge and watch the hillside leading to the pond. Perhaps a deer would come along to get a drink after being bedded down for most of the day and then feed all night. It was another evening of no sightings but it was still enjoyable to spend time with a friend in this beautiful setting. They both knew these kinds of days don't last forever but they do create memories which do.

As the sun disappeared behind the back ridge they packed up their gear and headed toward the cabin. The old lumber trail made the walk quite easy and their conversation was louder than the sound of their boots on the dirt and rocks. Who knows maybe tomorrow will prove to be the day when a big one comes ambling along and it can be brought home for dinner!

Chapter 8

Ernie tossed and turned all night because he couldn't get his mind to shut off on what he'd seen and what he thought should be done. Finally, he fell asleep but it was as if he just closed his eyes for 5 minutes when the alarm went off. He wanted to turn over and go back to sleep but he couldn't. He was there to hunt, not get his beauty rest!

What would today hold for the hunters? Only time would tell. The morning routine was the same, everyone up and a relatively quick breakfast of cereal or oatmeal, coffee and a donut. Lunches were packed and put in the backpacks. Getting dressed was easy, the temperatures were mild for a late fall day but today's forecast included rain. If there was a front moving in, it might mean the deer would be moving early, prior to the rain starting and it improved the chances of seeing some deer. So, included in the articles put in the backpack for the day, would be rain gear which could be put on over the camo to keep them dry if the rain actually started.

The clouds kept the sky darker for a longer time than normal because the sun was unable to cut through the heavy low-hanging clouds. When shooting light finally broke, the wind started to pick up and you could feel the moisture in the air. Rain was on its way, so hopefully the deer would come by prior to the rain. Unfortunately, there was no movement and the rain drops started to fall very lightly. Putting on the rain gear was easy but it meant quite a lot of movement which isn't good when you're sitting in a tree stand about 12 feet up in the air.

Jack had worn his rain pants when he left the cabin so he only had to put on the jacket and then climbed the ladder to his stand. He sat there leaning slightly forward in order to shelter his scope and keep the rain off the lens. He was warm and dry and intended to stay that way.

Jack scanned the area from the left to right, over and over, hoping to see something move. But what caught his eye was the light down at Stan's house. He saw the car heading out the driveway and then stop. The headlights were shining in the field across the road. The silence was broken by the sound of a rifle shot. Was that Stan? As Jack watched, he saw a flashlight shine across the road and whoever was holding it, crossed the road, went through the gate and stopped moving about 30 yards into the field. The light didn't move for about 20 minutes and then started back toward the gate, crossed the road and made its way to the barn.

It must have been Stan, who shot a deer using his headlights as spotlights before daylight because the legal hunting time is a half-hour before sunrise to a half-hour after sunset. It wasn't light enough to see much but if he really needed the meat to feed his family, what would anyone say? Poaching is illegal but if it meant the difference between having food on the table and going hungry, no one was going to turn them in! Jack certainly wouldn't. After a few minutes the headlights came on and the car turned out of the driveway and headed toward the paved road, Stan was off to work.

Meanwhile, back on the ridge daylight had finally broken and Jack suddenly, caught the glimpse of a flash of white. It was a deer, flicking its tail and looking the other way from where Jack was sitting. Maybe it would turn to come his way and not keep heading away.

What seemed like an eternity, he strained his eyes to see if the deer was a buck or doe? The head went down and then quickly raised back up, there was something which caught the deer's attention. It stood motionless, then stomped its foot to try to get whatever was making it nervous, move. Jack slowly raised his rifle and looked through the scope, getting the deer in his sights. It was a buck, it snorted and turned directly toward Jack and came bounding right at his stand. It was a small 4-point and probably a 2-year-old. He would pass on this one, even though he hadn't bagged a buck yet.

The buck pranced pass Jack without even looking up. It moved beyond his vision which was limited unless he turned his entire body to look around the tree and so it was gone. He sat there, excited but disappointed and could only think, that maybe another bigger buck would come along, later.

Ernie had gone to the front part of the property and near the bridge there was a ridge which gently started up and lead to the top of the left ridge which ran all the way to the back of the property. He saw a nice rub at the base of the hill and then proceeded to climb the ridge. Slowly he ascended, keeping an eye open for anything which might be ahead of him. He tried to be as quiet as possible but since it wasn't completely light when he started up, a couple of little limbs stung his face as they swiped across his cheek and he tripped over an unseen log in the darkness. He managed to keep his balance and just stood there for a moment before taking the next step.

Finally, shooting light broke and he avoided the low hanging branches and anything which might cause him to stumble or fall. He stopped every 10 feet or so and scanned the ridge ahead but didn't see anything. He was patient and kept the slow forward movement and it paid off. Suddenly, he saw a deer coming right down the middle of the ridge. Fortunately, he was standing behind a large oak tree and was blocked from the sight of the on-coming deer. He brought his gun up to his shoulder and leaned around the outside of the tree, trying to get his scope on the deer which was rapidly heading his way.

He got the crosshairs on the possible target and saw it was a doe. It continued down the ridge right past him without slowing down. He pulled his body back behind the tree and watched it without moving his head or body and it kept right on going. Suddenly, it stopped and looked back up the ridge, snorted a couple of times and then took off down the ridge on the dead run. Something must have spooked it or maybe it caught his scent since the wind was lightly blowing in her direction right past Ernie's hiding place.

He stood there, for a moment, putting his gun back down from his shoulder and then put the strap over his shoulder and prepared to step out to the left of the tree and head on up the ridge. Before, stepping out, he looked up the ridge and there was another deer running toward him. It was a buck! The antlers were easily visible and it was definitely a shooter but would he be able to get a shot? The buck was already at the tree before he could get his rife up to shoot. He quickly lifted it to his shoulder and pointed it at the escaping deer. He didn't have much time but he got the crosshairs on it and squeezed the trigger. It wasn't the kind of shot you want to take with a deer going away but it was the only one he had.

The buck took a couple of steps and then went down in a pile. He had apparently gotten a kill shot into the chest cavity and it blew up the heart. The deer was dead before hitting the ground. Now the real work began, as he had to drag it down the ridge and field dressed it. When he reached the bottom, he pulled it over to the creek to field dress it and then moved it into the creek to rinse the blood out of the carcass. He then pulled it into the weeds, found a stick to put inside the body cavity between the ribs and hid it so no one would find it and take it while he walked back to the cabin to get the truck and drive down to retrieve his trophy.

By the time he got the deer hung up in the outbuilding it was 9 am and his phone buzzed with several texts. Everyone was asking if it was him that shot and what he got. On a group text he said, Got a big 6! Am at the cabin. Good luck everyone!

Rex decided since he already had a nice buck, he would head in to help take care of Ernie's deer. He arrived and found Ernie sitting on the swing, just relaxing. Ernie waited for him to go in the basement and get out of his hunting gear. When Rex came out of the cabin, he had a bottle of water and sat down. Ernie started to share his success story. It was a much better message than yesterday. The rain had started to lightly fall but then picked up in intensity. Rex and Ernie got up and headed for the outbuilding to process the deer as it hung there, out of the rain.

When Rex finished, it was just like his for there was nothing left but the skeletal frame and all the meat was put in the freezer. So, it was 2 down and a few more to go before the freeze was full. Ernie lowered the skeleton onto the back of a 4-wheeler and headed toward the back of the property to discard it. He saw what remained of the other one, just scattered bones which were picked clean. He pulled up close and tossed the new one on the ground. He got on the 4-wheeler and turned to head back to the cabin. The rain was falling harder and it made the trail slick, so he had to go slower in order to not slide off the trail.

Jack and Patrick came off the ridge, looking like drowned rats and had not gotten a shot at anything.

Patrick had watched the other side of the ridge which was Stan's father-in-law's property. He thought that if Stan was going to poach deer for food for his family, then maybe they wouldn't mind if he legally shot something which was near the top of the ridge. Unfortunately, he didn't see anything. Jack came over and whistled for him and Patrick walked over to where Jack was waiting and they headed down the ridge together in a steady rain.

Only Wayne was still out in the rain but he gave up too and headed down to the cabin. Maybe it would clear up later and everyone could get back out. The rain would make their entrance very quiet but it also meant the deer could move and not be heard when walking along in the wet leaves. Since the deer lived in the wild the rain didn't really affect them but often they would bed down under the pines or in a dense undergrowth to wait for the rain to quit and then get up to feed especially if their morning feeding pattern was interrupted.

Chapter 9

The week had passed quickly and the hunting trip/ vacation was coming to an end. Only one more day and then it was back home and returning to the daily grind of work. However, the hunting season lasted 3 weeks so the weekends would allow for some additional time in the woods, hunting the elusive creatures. You have to wonder where they go when hunting season comes in. They can't climb trees, hide under rocks, take vacations to somewhere else, they just don't seem to be around, but if you're persistent enough, spend time in the woods and are a good scout, you will find them.

The final day of this hunt was without incident but no one saw a buck. There was a small group of 5 does which moved around and was seen by a couple of the guys but as the day wore on, the enthusiasm waned. By noon, everyone had had enough and came back to the cabin. It was time to pack up their belongings, clean the cabin and head home.

After the vacuum was run, dishes washed and put away, the refrigerator was checked and anything which wouldn't last was tossed in the garbage. All the beds were stripped and the dirty towels, dishrags and dirty clothes were collected so they could be taken home and washed. On the return trip, all of these would be returned and reused.

Everyone but Rex pulled away by 3 o'clock and he decided to drop over to the Jones' house and check on Jeremiah and Betty. As he pulled onto the 2-track road leading over to their place, a van came up behind him and seemed to be in a hurry to get past. When he turned into the lane which led to the Jones' driveway, the van turned right behind him. As he pulled into the driveway the van went past him, heading toward the Black's place. A woman was driving and it looked like a man sitting in the passenger's seat. It was Joyce and Junior, coming back from town.

Rex stopped the car and Killer; the dog came barking from around the back of the house. Rex got out, stood by the car and the dog came over to greet him. After petted him, he headed up onto the porch. Peering through the window there was no one to be seen, so he knocked on the door and took a step back to wait. In a short time, the door opened and Betty was standing there. *I was getting ready to head home and wanted to drop over to see how you folks were,"* said Rex. Betty replied, *"Well, Jeremiah is at the hospital and they think he's had a stroke! I've been going every day and he seems to be getting along well. They say he might go to rehab tomorrow and after a few weeks, be able to come home. The boys were called but aren't coming since he's getting along ok."*

Rex was surprised because he hadn't heard an ambulance come up past the cabin but maybe they didn't use the siren when coming to pick him up. His unasked question was answered as Betty said, *"They didn't come for him, I drove him to the hospital two days ago."* *"What can I do to help?"* Rex asked. Betty said, "*Nothing. I am fine. My sister-in-law Carol and niece Joyce are stopping in to check on me.*"

"Remember, you have my number if I can help in any way," Rex reminded her. "*I'll probably be back at the cabin next weekend and I'll stop by to see you,*" he said as he turned to go back to the truck. "*Oh,*" he said, "*I just had a woman and a man follow me here and head back the lane to the Black's house*". Betty nodded her head, "*That was probably Joyce, she works on Saturday cleaning houses and takes Junior to the movie. It's a Saturday ritual for them and gives them a break from being stuck at home all the time. Their routine is always the same, after she finishes her work, she'll pick him up from the movie house and they'll go to the local diner for a bite of supper before heading home.*"

Everyone loved Joyce and knew Junior was harmless, even though he was a big young man! He would always go over to the little ones who were sitting in highchairs and pat them on the head and talk to them. The children were not afraid of him and never cried when he came close. The parents knew his intentions were never harmful. He was just a big kid at heart, due to his mental limitations.

Rex wanted to ask about the cave at the back of the Black's property but thought maybe it would be best not to mention it. He headed back to the cabin, made sure everything was locked up and the circuit breakers were off. He exited the cabin got in the truck and as he drove down the lane, he glanced up on the ridge to the right. About half way up, there stood a deer! He stopped the truck and continued to watch it, as it just walked along and seemed quite at ease. Maybe it knew the hunters were leaving and it was safe until they returned. He let his foot off the brake, crossed the bridge and pulled to a stop past the gate. He got out to lock the gate and after doing so, got back in the truck and headed for home.

As he drove back he began to think about what the week had revealed. How could they do anything about the items in the cave and if they reported it to the authorities, what would they do? Afterall, Rex was an outsider and this wasn't his home, he only owned property there. Besides, if the police went to the Blacks what would they find, they could easily have moved the items or maybe hidden the entrance to the cave, so it couldn't be searched. Then, you would have to wonder what repercussions there would be on the part of the Blacks toward them, because they would know the information had to have come from Rex. Lots of questions and very few clear answers!

Meanwhile back at the Black's property, Ballard, John Henry and Junior were taking action to hide the entrance to the cave. Using the tractor, with a front-end loader, they moved some large rocks close to the entrance, so that it was not identifiable as the cave's entry point. They also piled some dead limbs from trees among them making it look like a natural area on the hill. All of this could be removed later and it would be easy access once again. They weren't sure what if anything might happen, but they were taking steps to avoid detection. They were quite uneasy knowing someone had been down there and saw what was stashed away in the cave.

After finishing their task of hiding the cave's entrance, everyone gathered around the kitchen table to collectively decide what was to be done next. As they came up with various ideas, Joyce spoke up, "*Let's go over to Callahan's cabin and pay them a visit. It will serve as a warning to not bother us again! I will take Junior and we'll be back in a little while.*" Sounded like a good plan to the rest and so Joyce and Junior got up and headed for the van.

Arriving at the gate, it was locked but they had a pair of bolt cutters in the van and Junior made short work of cutting it. The chain was released and the gate swung open. Joyce drove the van through the open gate and Junior closed it. They drove up to the cabin and Junior got out and proceeded to put his size 14 boot to the door and it busted the door wide open, as the frame split on the inside. They now had access to the entire cabin.

The television was the first object taken down and put on the porch. The microwave would be next and even the telephone was taken. The guns which were on display were gathered and removed. There didn't seem to be anything else upstairs, so they proceeded to put all of this into the van. Then it was down to the basement. There were tools and a 4-wheeler which could be added to the stolen items. As Junior gathered the tools, Joyce drove the van around the cabin to the basement door. Junior opened the door from the inside and the tools were loaded into the van. The 4-wheeler would be ridden by Junior back through the valley, up and over the ridge and taken to a perfect hiding spot.

Joyce proceeded to the gate. put the chain back without the lock and pulled out to head home. The message had been sent and they would just have to wait until they knew how Rex and his family reacted. If they were smart, nothing would happen but if they wanted to pursue something, it would only get worse! Afterall, the last people who lived there had their house burn to the ground!

The van load of items was put into a safe hiding spot in the barn until they could be taken to any number of pawn shops in the nearby towns, where Joyce was a regular customer. She knew she couldn't take too many items all at once but a limited number could go each month, with a story about needing extra money for various bills. The pawn shop owner knew not to ask questions but did offer some decent prices for the items she would bring. This provided Junior with movie money and Joyce with discretionary funds to do with as she pleased and that included giving generously to her church. She had almost single-handedly given enough for the choir to have new robes and everyone was so complimentary of her generosity. If they only knew the truth!

Junior rode the 4-wheeler back through the valley, up the ridge and down the other side and onto the gated lane which went back to the barn and house. About half way between the gate and cave was a metal shed and he stopped, opened the doors and rode it inside. He then closed up the shed and walked to the house. This shed had not been noticed by Ernie when he discovered the cave. It appeared to be a large storage shed for hay, because there were numerous bales piled around the outside. When you opened the doors there were bales stacked up blocking the entrance giving the impression of it being full of hay. If you got past the façade of bales there was a work shop where John Henry would refurbish and paint the bicycles, motorcycles and scooters. After he finished his painting and detailing, no one would be able to recognize their stolen vehicles. His plan was to collect a few, do the work and then trailer them to flea markets in other towns where he could get a pretty penny for them, even though there was no available title. Sometimes what's legal or illegal isn't really an issue for some individuals when purchasing certain things.

The items which made their way to the farm and away again, provided a pretty good extra income for the whole family. Besides, a new microwave or television set every now and then, wasn't a bad benefit for everyone! The whole operation was spearheaded by the most unlikely person, Joyce. All the others were merely willing participants!

Chapter 10

Friday afternoon meant heading to the cabin for a couple of days of deer hunting since there was still another full week left in the season. Little did Rex know what awaited him. As he got to the gate, he noticed the lock had been cut and was laying on the ground. The chain had been put back through the gate, so it looked as if it were secure but it wasn't. He pushed the gate open and headed for the cabin, wondering what he might find. When he pulled up and looked, there was the front door standing wide open. He got out and stepped through the door to scan the room. He looked to his right and there was an empty space on the wall where the TV used to hang, only the brackets remained. He looked to his left and the gun racks were empty. His heart sank thinking about the valuable weapons he had collected over the years but now were gone. He turned his attention toward the kitchen and there was no microwave on the counter and even the phone was gone!

He went upstairs but nothing seemed to be out of place and then he went down to the basement. The door was partially open and only the riding lawnmower occupied the space in front of the door. The 4-wheeler which was supposed to be setting there, was gone! The tools which normally covered the workbench were also nowhere to be seen and various yard tools which normally hung on hooks on the wall were noticeably absent. Whoever broke in certainly knew what they wanted, it seemed!

Rex went back upstairs and opened the credenza to see if the movies were still there. They were but the DVD player was gone, along with the cord which connected it to the TV. He guessed the thieves didn't like their assortment of movies or didn't see them when they hastily removed the DVD player. He then took a second look around but didn't notice anything else missing. His next action was to dial 9-1-1 and report the break in. He went out and dejectedly sat down on the swing and waited for the arrival of the police.

There were no lights flashing or sirens to be heard when the cruiser pulled up in front of the cabin. The officer got out, put his hand on his gun and spoke to Rex. *"Are you the one who called about the break in?"* Rex remained seated and replied, *"Yes I am. Name is Rex Callahan, I bought this place this year and we built this cabin so we would have a place to hunt and spend some family time. Everything has been great until today when I arrived. Someone broke in and took some of our belongings that's why I called you."*

The officer, named Heath walked over and peered through the door. He said, *"Doesn't look like they did any damage inside, but they certainly busted this door."* He continued, *"You say they took some items?"* Rex nodded his head and handed him an itemized list of things he noted were no longer where they belonged. Heath took a moment to review the list and said, "*Well, you have joined a growing list of victims in our area. I don't know that we have much hope in recovering anything but we'll look into it. Did you have your name on any of these things or have the serial numbers of any of them written down? This could help in locating them, especially if they show up at our station.*" Rex responded, "*You're right but I didn't make a complete list or etch my name on any of them. Guess I've learned a valuable lesson. I hope my insurance will cover replacing them.*" The officer nodded and said, "*Most likely they will, since you've reported the break in and we'll file a report. You can get the official report next week or we can fax it to you.*" Rex thanked him for the help and gave him the fax number at the office.

Heath looked around outside and noticed some 4-wheeler tracks leading from the basement door and back through the valley. He said he was going to take a walk and see if he could find anything helpful. Rex sat back down in the swing and watched the officer disappear into the back woods. He was gone for about 30 minutes and then returned. *"It looked like the tracks led up and over the ridge. I think the Blacks live back that way, so I might take a ride back that way and see if they saw or heard anything,"* said Heath.

Rex spoke up, *"You will need to be careful they aren't the friendliest of folks, but maybe you already know that. I certainly wasn't welcome when I visited and when one of my sons was hunting last week, he went over the ridge, and said he saw a cave that was full of all kinds of stuff."* *"What kind of stuff?"* Asked the officer. Rex knew he had opened pandora's box, so he might as well tell him what Ernie had said.

"There were TV's, microwaves, computers, laptops, telephone answering machines, bicycles, motorcycles, scooters and apparently buckets full of jewelry," answered Rex. He continued, *"Junior saw my son Ernie and went after his dad but Ernie hightailed it over the ridge and back here. We were sitting in the*

cabin when old man Black came storming in and threatened us for being on his property.

Heath took out his tablet, wrote something on it and then said, "*Thanks. I'll take a careful look around and keep in mind what you said about them not wanting anybody snooping around.*" With that he got in the cruiser turned around and was talking on his radio when he left the cabin to drive down the lane.

Heath drove up the two-lane road, turned onto the double driveway, passed the Jones' house and came slowly rolling to a stop at the Black's house. He was met by Ballard, who called out, "*What do you want?*" "*We ain't done nothing, so why you here?*" Heath, stayed in the car and responded, "*I had a call from Callahan about a break in and there were tracks leading over the ridge toward your place. I wondered if you had heard or seen anything suspicious recently?*" Ballard shook his head no. The officer then said, "*Do you mind if I get out and take a look around?*" Gruffly, Ballard said, "*Yes I do! If you want to look around,*" *you'd better bring a search warrant! Now get off my property!"*

Heath knew the Black's reputation so he backed up and headed out. However, this wasn't going to be the end. He got on the radio and called in to the station to report what had happened and asked the captain for advice on what to do next.

When Heath got back to the station, the captain called him in for a full report. After retelling what Callahan had stated, the captain said, "*Let's go see the judge and get a search warrant! If he wants to play hardball, we'll do just that!*" The two left the station and drove over to Judge Miller's house and knocked on the door. The housekeeper opened the door and informed them the Judge and his wife were out of town for the weekend but would be back on Monday. They thanked her and went back to the station. It would have to wait until Monday and then they'd go back to the Black's place for aaround.

Rex called Ernie and Jack to report what had happened and they brought some hand tools to repair the front door. It would be an hour or so before they could get there, so Rex closed up the basement and went upstairs to wait. He slipped into one of the recliners and before he knew it was sound asleep. He was awakened by the sound of a car door slamming. The boys had were there and came in. Taking a long look around they just shook their heads in disgust! "*Who would do this?*" they said in unison. Rex just pointed in the direction of the Blacks. "*If what you said was true, I think they did this as a warning!*" said Rex. "*But I called the cops and an officer was here and told me he would go over to check things out. Guess, we'll wait and see if anything comes of it.*"

The frame on the door had been busted so after repairing the frame, another step of safety was added. A dead bolt they had purchased was installed. A hole was drilled for the deadbolt to fit into. It went through the frame and into the wall of the cabin. It would take a lot more force to get in the next time, if there was a next time.

As dark settled in, there wasn't much to do at the cabin, so they decided to ride into town and have a bite of dinner. The boys had also purchased a new lock and keys, so they closed the gate and put the new lock in place before heading out. On their way, they happened to see Stan out in the front yard where he was calling the children in for dinner. They stopped and Rex called out, "*We got broken into this week, did you see anything suspicious or hear anything?*" Stan walked over to the car as it sat in the roadway, "*No, but there seems to have been a lot of that going on. Wish they would find who's behind all these break ins and get them stopped. I worry about my wife being here alone all day but so far, we've been spared.*" Rex thanked him and the car began to edge forward as they headed towards town. Jack said, "*It's awfully quiet around here most of the time, but it's not unusual for folks who keep their doors and windows closed, to not hear anything. We certainly can't hear much that happens on the road when we're at the cabin."*

Dinner was rather quiet, except for some discussions about where they were going to hunt in the morning. Rex thought it might be best to avoid the right ridge which connected with the Blacks, so he would go to the back of the property where the valley ended at the saddle and Jack and Ernie could spread out on the right ridge and maybe catch something coming up the hill or along the side in one of the flats. It sounded like a good plan and they agreed.

When they got back to the cabin, it was time for another movie and then off to bed. This was the normal routine each evening they were at the cabin, after spending the day in the woods. Sometimes, before watching the movie, they would get the discs from the cameras to see if there were any deer showing up. The feeders usually drew in turkeys, deer and other critters, including a big black bear, which appeared on the camera. Movement triggers the camera and the images are captured for them to review at a later time.

Chapter 11

Saturday morning meant getting up before sunrise and getting ready for a day in the woods. Breakfast with coffee would suffice and a peanut butter and jelly sandwich would be an excellent lunch. Water and a soda would complete the menu, along with something for a mid-morning snack like a granola bar or a moon pie. All three of them prepared their lunch, snacks and drinks and were ready to head out before daylight began to break. There was no 4-wheeler to bring a deer in but that would be a bridge to cross if anyone got one.

Each of them reached their destination before first light, so the flashlights helped. They climbed the ladders and got situated, waiting for light to quietly edge the darkness from the woods. It wasn't long and the once distant trees and terrain began to come into focus. If anything moved, it would be seen by a keen eye and as they looked around there were some new signs to be noted. Rex saw a new rub on the trail leading along the lower rim of the saddle. Maybe the buck would come by again this morning. He patiently waited, keeping an eye in the direction of the rub and trail but nothing ever came along the route.

Jack notice a fresh scrape as the light began to break from the eastern sky and it got his blood flowing. It hadn't been there last week when he hunted from the tree stand. It was only about 10 yards away and if anything came to it, he had a great view and open shot. Ernie had gone on out the ridge and was watching down the side toward Stan's house, hoping something would come up to the top and he might get a shot. He could see the field down by the road and also see Stan's house.

Ernie's attention was drawn to Stan's house as he saw Stan and one of his sons exit the house and begin to walk across the road to the open field. If anything was standing out there, it would surely be spooked and come running up the side of the hill. He sat anxiously, waiting to hear the coming deer. Minutes turned to a hour and nothing! However, he did hear what sounded like muffled voices. He slowly stood up and looked over the rim of the ridge and was surprised to see Stan and the boy slowly edging their way up the hill. Before reaching the top, they veered off to the right, which would eventually take them to where Jack was set up, if they went that far. He kept his eye on them as they quietly moved away from him. He wondered if they saw him and that's why they veered off. As he watched, they slipped along but disappeared occasionally among the trees. About 150 yards away they stopped and sat down on the side of the hill, behind a cluster of trees. It would be a good vantage point for anything coming along below the top of the ridge or making its way up from the field below. It was not a good situation for Ernie because they had effectively cut off anything that could come from Jack's direction, unless it was on the other side of the ridge and was actually on their property.

Ernie sat there for about a half an hour and decided to move down the ridge toward the cabin. This way there was no way anyone could get shot if a deer came up between where he was and where Stan and his son were. Safety is always the best choice. He quietly slipped down to the ground and took small steps in the leaves, trying not to make any noise. He was doing well until his foot slipped and down, he went with a rather loud crash in the leaves. He sat there collecting himself and then got to his feet to continue his journey. Hopefully he hadn't scared anything away and the other hunters didn't hear him. He came to the edge of the ridge which began to descend to the front of the property and the creek. He took up his position, getting quite comfortable on the ground as he leaned back against a large oak tree. He knew he could sit here the rest of the day, if he wished but it might be difficult to stay awake since it was so comfortable. He didn't stay awake!

Jack was scouring the hill for the sign of movement since the scrape was fresh. About mid-morning his patience was rewarded as he caught a deer moving between the trees. It was walking along and kept looking back over its shoulder, something must have spooked it. It is a theory by an experienced hunter that when a deer is leery, if 2 of its 3 senses are confirmed it will run away. The 3 senses are hearing, seeing and smelling. The doe wasn't running so whatever had pushed it his way didn't spook it. He didn't know Stan and his son were back toward where she was glancing. As the deer closed in on the scrape, Jack saw it was a big doe and she came right to the scrape, stood there peed in it then walked through the scrape and headed toward Jack. This would let the buck know if she was in estrous and if so, he would come searching as soon as he revisited the scrape. Jack was getting excited to have seen this and only imaged what the big guy might look like.

About a half hour later, he heard something in the leaves and turned his attention toward where the sound originated. He saw the buck but it wasn't a big one, it was a spike and he was heading right for the scrape. Surely, he wasn't the one who made the scrape, but he certainly knew where it was and was coming to check it out. He did seem a bit skittish as he walked in. Maybe he was invading the big boy's territory and the dominant buck wouldn't approve of any such actions. The spike came over and smelled the ground and then headed off in the direction the doe had gone but at a much quicker pace than she did when leaving. The spike hadn't been gone but a few minutes when suddenly, a massive buck appeared from what seemed to be out of nowhere! He proceeded directly toward the scrape to check it out. He then, lifted his head and the antlers shone in the sunlight. They were massive and there were plenty of them! He then began to trot toward the direction the doe and spike had gone. Little did he know, he was heading right toward Jack's stand

and Jack was ready. As the distance closed from where he first saw him to about 20 yards, Jack put the cross hairs on the buck's chest and squeezed the trigger. The silence was broken by the sound of the rifle and the buck, jumped straight up, tucked his tail and started running back in the direction of the scrape. He went about 50 yards when he did a nose-dive into a cluster of bushes. He didn't make another move but Jack waited about 20 minutes before getting down to go to check out the downed deer.

When he got to it, he heard something moving in the leaves beyond where he was standing. It was Stan and his son, coming to sound of the gunshot. Although they were on Rex's property, there was no problem for them being there. How many times does a youngster get to see a deer taken while hunting? Besides, it could be a real learning experience for the little guy as he watched Jack field dress the deer.

Ernie's nap was interrupted by the shot and he perked up and began to look around. He didn't see anything but a couple of squirrels scampering along the side of the ridge below him. He wondered if it was Jack or Stan who shot. Rather than send a text, he got up, stretched and started to move along the ridge back toward where Jack was hunting. He did slip higher on the ridge in order to see where Stan and his son had stopped but they were nowhere to be seen. He then picked up the pace and headed toward Jack. It wasn't long before he saw all 3 of them, with Jack working on a downed deer. The other two were simply standing there watching. It was a good sight.

As Ernie drew closer, they heard the noise in the leaves and turned their attention that direction. When they saw Ernie, they waved him over and as he walked close, he sat his gun against a tree, he asked, "*Who got this big guy, was it your son, Stan?*" He replied, "*No it was your brother! I've seen this guy all fall but he has eluded me and today, he was in the wrong place at the wrong time! Guess your brother's homework paid off.*"

Having finished the job of field dressing the buck, Jack took out a rope and tied it to the rack and looked at Ernie and said, *"You ready to help me drag this guy down to the cabin?"* Ernie smiled and grabbed his gun and took hold of the loop Jack had made with the rope on the buck's antlers. "*Well, we'll leave the rest of the ridge to you two and we hope one of you can get a shot at a good one,*" said Jack. *"Thanks for coming over and offering to help,"* he said as he grabbed his gun and the rope. The brothers started down the ridge and the drag would be easy with the leaves on the ground and it was downhill all the way! All they had to be careful of was to not let the deer's antlers slide into the back of their legs or ankles.

Stan and his son headed back over the ridge to spend some more time in the woods. Who knows maybe another deer will come along and they can get a shot at one too? It didn't matter to them if it was a buck or a doe, it would be something to remember for a lifetime for a little guy to be able to shoot his first deer, while hunting with his father. They repositioned themselves just below the top of the ridge and watched one of the flats which ran along side of it. Just before dark, the guys back at the cabin heard a gunshot from up on the ridge. A nice doe had come along and Matt got to take a shot. He didn't hit it with a kill shot but it was bleeding and a blood trail was easy to follow if the light wasn't lost. About 15 minutes later, a second shot was heard and they guys wondered if Stan or the boy finished off the wounded deer. Now they had to drag it down to the field and off to the barn where it could be dressed and processed. Dad would have to do the majority of the dragging and all of the field dressing but Matt had gotte n his first deer!

It had been a great day hunting and there was work to do in the outbuilding as they needed to de-bone the deer and dispose of the skeletal remains. It would be dark before the job was done but the skeleton was put in the back of the truck and taken out to join the other ones back on the valley floor. After putting the venison in the freezer, they headed into the house to have a bite of dinner. Vicky had made a pan of lasagna to be warmed up for dinner and Rex had put it in before the boys made it down from the ridge. They had called him on the phone and reported their success. So, all they had to do was wash up, get out the plates and silverware and enjoy a delicious home-cooked meal, thanks to Mom!

Since all 3 had gotten a deer, no one wanted to get up Sunday morning to hunt, so they slept in. It was daylight before they began to stir in the cabin. They thought it was nice to not have to get up and face the cold. They hadn't checked the weather report and much to their surprise there was a skiff of snow covering the ground. Wow, when there is snow on the ground, it seems like you can see forever in the woods and you can easily spot a brown deer against a white background, even at several hundred yards. That applies to all the other creatures which live in the woods and usually are not seen.

After a leisurely breakfast, they packed up the venison from all 3 of the deer in the freezer and put it in multiple ice chests in order to take it home. This would ensure some good eating for quite a number of meals in the coming months! After securing the cabin and turning off the breakers, they were ready to go. They headed down the lane to the gate with Rex trailing, so he could lock the gate after the boys opened it.   After securing the lock on the gate, Rex turned toward the Jones's house to check on Jeremiah and Betty.

He pulled in the drive way and was surprised to not be met by Killer. He stopped the truck and got out. As he stepped up on the porch, he heard Killer barking from inside the house as he came running to the door because Rex had knocked on the door. It was just a minute or less before Betty came to see who was there. She saw Rex through the window and smiled. She opened the door and Killer stuck his nose against Rex's leg as if to check that it was really him. The dog then began to wag his tail and backed up. Betty invited him in and they went into the living room. There was Jeremiah sitting in a recliner, a tv-tray was placed beside him and what looked like the remnants of breakfast were scattered on the plate. The coffee cup still had steaming coffee in it and he looked at Rex with a slight smile on his face.

Jeremiah spoke first, "*Look Ma, our boy has come to visit!*" Betty looked somewhat embarrassed as she looked over at Rex and just shook her head. Then she said, "*Since the stroke, he doesn't always remember everyone and get confused if anyone comes. Please forgive the mistake.*" Rex smiled and said, "*No problem. If he thinks I'm one of your boys and its helpful, let it be whatever he thinks. It's an honor to be associated with you folks.*" Betty smiled and said, "*Thank you.*" Then she added, "*Why don't you sit down for a spell?*" Rex did.

They exchanged small talk and then Rex asked, "*Are your sons going to come to visit you all?*" There was an uncomfortable silence and she shook her head to indicate, no. Rex couldn't conceive how sons could stay away when they were really needed. Betty could certainly use some help and their father didn't deserve to be ignored at a time like this. He wondered why they wouldn't come but didn't want to pry. He just said, "*I'm sorry they aren't already here or heading home. Maybe they'll come later.*" Betty just looked at him and smiled.

They visited for a little while and then Rex said he needed to head for home. He asked if she would like a little venison, since they had gotten 3 nice deer. She thought for a moment and said, "*Are you sure you want to give some of it away?*" Rex smiled and said, "*Of course, we can't eat a whole deer and sharing it is what makes the hunting worthwhile. Just stay there while I go out and get some out of the ice chest in the truck.*" He walked out to the truck and was going through the pieces of meat in the ice chest when the van he had seen last week came up the lane and stopped at the end of the driveway. The window went down on the passenger's side and the lady driver called out, "*What are you doing here and what's that in the back of your truck?*" Rex turned in her direction and held up some packages of venison and said, "*Deer meat, I'm giving it to Miss Betty and Mr. Jeremiah.*" Rex then asked, "*May I ask who you are?*" She bristled at the question but responded, "*I'm Betty's niece, Joyce. And, who are you?*" She knew who he was so his answer didn't surprise her when he said, "*I'm Rex Callahan and we bought the Moore farm and have been hunting this fall. We built a cabin and plan to use it as our hunting lodge and a place for the family to have family outings. Unfortunately, we had a break-in but we aren't worried.*" He paused for a moment and then continued, "*Did you all happen to hear anything strange or see someone ride a 4-wheeler over the ridge toward your property? The police officer saw the tracks going that way.*" She responded, "*Sorry to hear about your bad luck. We didn't see or hear anything.*" "*Ok,*" replied

Rex, as he turned to go back into the house. The conversation was over and the van drove on down the dual lane toward the Black's house.

Betty was pleased with the steaks and chops and put them in the freezer for a future meal. She thanked him. He then said, "*I guess I met your niece Joyce, she stopped to see what I was doing at your house. I told her I was giving you some venison and asked if they had seen or heard anything last week.*" He continued, "*When they broke in to the house, they took a 4-wheeler and rode it over the ridge which goes down to their property. She said, they hadn't and then drove off.*"

Betty looked at him and said, "*They're really private and don't like anyone to be on their property. I don't know what's up with them but I just don't ask. Not any of my business, even though they're family. Best to not go nosing around where you're not wanted! Don't you agree?*" Rex responded, "*You're absolutely right.*" "*I am going now, hope you all enjoy the venison and I will be back around probably next week. Remember, call me, if there is something I can help with. My daughter-in-law is a nurse and would gladly help if needed."* With that he opened the door and walked to the truck.

The property was working out great and the hunting was good. Beyond hunting season, there would be some great family gatherings and wonderful memories would be created for every member in the family, from the adults to the grandkids. Maybe in time the neighbors would be friends and the holidays could include them, especially the Jones. He didn't think the Blacks would ever come around, but who knows! Stan's family could be a good connection, since the grandkids and their kids were close in age.As with everything, it's just one day at a time and you just have to let things happen as they will.

Chapter 12

Monday morning came and the police department was stirring with excitement as they awaited the search warrant for the Black property. The captain had called the judge's office to request the needed warrant and sent Heath over to pick it up. Judge Miller had signed it and the secretary had it laying on her desk when the young officer walked in.

"I'm here for the warrant to search the Black's farm," Heath informed the secretary. *"Yes, here it is,"* she responded. *"Thank you,"* he said as he picked it up and turned to leave. *"Best be careful going out there and I wouldn't go alone,"* were her words to him. He thought about what she said and when he got back to the station, he walked into the captain's office. *"How about several officers going with me and maybe we ought to ask the State Police to get in on this,"* Heath inquired? *I've been warned by several people about the Blacks and there just might be trouble. What do you think, captain?"*

The captain picked up the phone and called the State Police post and talked to the commander with his back turned to Heath, so he couldn't hear the conversation. He hung up the phone and said, "*They will be joining us in about an hour. In the meantime, get the officers together for a meeting and we'll discuss our strategy for going out there and searching the property.*" Heath turned to exit and spread the word about a meeting for all the officers who were on duty that day.

They gathered and waited for the captain to enter the room. He went directly to the podium in the front of the room. "*Gentlemen,*" he began, "*We have a warrant for the Ballard Black farm and are going out there in force. The State Highway Patrol will be joining us, in case there is any trouble. If you know this family, they have quite a reputation for trouble in this community! Make sure you have on your vests and helmets and arm yourselves; handguns and shotguns are the order of the day. We'll go in procession, I'll be leading so have on your lights but no sirens. Upon arrival, spread yourselves out so you have the house surrounded. Heath will deliver the warrant to Black and if there are no issues, we'll begin a systematic search of the property from the house to the barn, any outbuildings and look for any places which they might have tried to cover up or disguise. Everyone understand?"* There was a collective nod by all the officers. The captain then finished with, "*Ok, dismissed!*" As they stood up and began to exit the room, the captain offered these final words: "*We'll be assembling out front in about 20 minutes and heading out of town, so don't be late! Got it?*"

It was quite a sight to see the police cruisers with lights on racing out of town. They got to the lane which lead to the Callahan farm and to the double driveway at the Jones' farm. Waiting for them were 4 state highway officers, with lights flashing. The captain got out and spoke to the Highway Patrol officer and then got back in his car and they all headed toward the Black's farm.

They passed the Jones' house and when they reached the Black's property, they turned into the drive and spread out in the front yard and a couple of the cruisers went around behind the house. Heath got out of his cruiser and began to walk toward the front door. He called out, *"Mr. Black, I have a warrant to search your property and I am delivering it to you."* He had hardly finished his speech when the front door cracked open and a gun poked out and fired a shot right into the chest of the young officer. He fell back in the grass and lay motionless on the ground.

What followed was a volley of gun fire from the officers which took out the windows, passed through the clapboard walls and turned the door into what looked like swiss cheese! Return fire sporadically came from the windows on each side of the door, resulting in bullet holes appearing in the windshields and open door windows being shattered. The officers were using the vehicles for protection but one officer went down. A bullet had struck him in the shoulder and he sat down on the ground, leaned against the side of the cruiser while grabbing the wound. Another officer came over and looked at the wound and got on his phone to call 9-1-1 to request an ambulance with the explanation *"Officer down!"*

As gun shots were exchanged from both sides the first causality in the house was Junior who was firing from one of the windows. He fell back onto the floor a bullet had struck him in the forehead and made a large hole in the back of his skull. Taking his place was Ballard, who tried to pick out an officer and get revenge for the death of his son. He kept firing but never quite found the mark. John Henry was at the other window and fired occasionally; he had been hit but not fatally. The women had retreated to the kitchen and were hiding by the pantry. They heard the officers behind the house and armed themselves. Carol cracked the kitchen door and fired a couple of shots in the direction of the officers. Her shots were followed by a volley of bullets which splintered the door and struck her several times, sending her to the floor with blood flowing from what would be fatal wounds.

Joyce screamed but didn't pick up the weapon her mother had put on the floor by her. She started crying and slumped on the floor. With no additional shots coming from the kitchen, the officers in the back of the house cautiously moved toward the door and entered with guns ready to take down anyone who resisted. They saw Carol and told her to put her hands on the floor and lay down. She complied. One officer went over to put her in handcuffs, while the other officers slipped from the kitchen into the dining room checking for anyone and then came to front room. He saw Junior lying on the floor apparently dead from a shot to the head. Ballard was slumped over at the window having been hit with several bullets in the chest, arms and neck. He made no movements. In the corner of the room was John Henry, who was sitting on the floor with a handgun pointed at the officer. "*Put it down!*" the officer commanded. He just sat there, continuing to point the weapon in an aggressive pose. "*Put the gun down!*" he repeated.

John Henry, tried to talk but his speech was halting because of the bullet which had hit his lungs. He finally got out his final words, "*I'm not going back to that hell-hole called a prison.*" He squeezed the trigger but missed his target, the officer didn't and John Henry's head slumped to his chest and the gun fell from his hand. He was dead. He had been given an opportunity to surrender but he refused, which resulted in his demise. When are people going to learn to comply with an officer's command and avoid becoming a victim? It wasn't police brutality it was a actually a matter of non-compliance and stupidity!

Since the house was now secured, they took Joyce out to one of the cruisers and put her in the back seat. She could wait there and maybe she would provide some information, so they didn't take her back to the station. The search was about to begin and the captain came over to the cruiser, opened the door and asked if she wanted to offer any help in where to begin looking. She just stared at him but didn't speak. It would up to them to find something if there was anything there but she knew there was! The house was searched and the televisions, computers and phones were gathered and put into the van which had arrived from the station. Also, the CSI van was there and the medical examiner was on the scene to make some preliminary determinations regarding what had taken place.

Heath had not been injured, other than the bruise to his chest from the bullet which Black fired at him. He had laid on his back for the duration of the fire-fight which lasted about 10 minutes. The officer who had been wounded was taken to the hospital in the ambulance and fortunately he didn't have a life-threatening wound. All of the Black family was dead, except for Joyce who apparently didn't take part in any of the shooting. Four hearses came to transport their bodies back to the medical examiner's office for a closer examination which would be made as part of the official report.

As the officers walked away from the house toward the back of the property, they walked through the gate and came to the metal shed. It appeared to be just a storage shed for hay, since the bales blocked the door from the inside. However, one of the officers pushed on them and amazingly they moved. He then began to pull some bales out of the way and behind them there was an open work area which served as John Henry's paint shop. Sitting in the middle of the room was a 4-wheeler which had been masked to be repainted and some of the parts were scattered around on the counter.

Other officers walked on past and noticed the hill where there were rocks and limbs piled around but it looked rather suspicious. They moved some of the limbs and tried to move the rocks but they were too heavy. The smaller ones were tossed aside and it looked like there was an opening behind the larger rocks. Since the tractor with the front-end loader was down at the barn, one officer went down to get it in order to remove some of the large rocks. When he got back, moving them with the front-end loader was easy and they exposed the opening to what looked like a cave. It was actually an old coal mine which had played out some years ago.

After clearing away all the debris which blocked the entrance the officers shined their lights into the darkness and there were all kinds of items. Heath had made his way back and when he walked in his first comment was "*Oh, yeah! Callahan said they saw all this stuff and I'll bet it will be the solution to all of those break-ins we couldn't solve. Let's get the van back here and fill it up, so we can take it all back to the stationhouse.*" Reed, one of the other officers, walked toward the house and informed the van driver of the loot which was in the cave and he needed to go back to the mine so all of it could be loaded and taken to the station. By the time they finished it was almost dark and the van was totally full. Some of the smaller items had to be put in the cruisers but finally everything was collected. They pulled away from the bullet riddled house and headed back to town. Betty stood on the porch watching as the cars pulled past her house and onto the two-lane road.

Monday turned out to be quite a memorable day for the police force and the shootout at the Black farm would certainly go down in the annals of the community's memorable history.

Joyce had been transported to the jail and put in a cell where she was going to be held until an official charge was filed. Her court appearance was scheduled the next day, when Judge Miller would have her arraignment to set bail or keep her in custody. A public defender was offered to her on Monday evening and she accepted. He came to see her and talked about what she could plead regarding the pending charges. He promised to be in court with her the next day at the hearing.

Chapter 13

The news of Monday's events spread like wildfire in the little town and there was quite a crowd who came to the courthouse and filled all the seats to see and hear the proceedings. Judge Miller sat at the high desk in his black judicial robe and Joyce was led into the courtroom in an orange jump suit with chains on her wrists and ankles. It was quite a picture for this beloved citizen, who had some serious charges being levied at her.

The bailiff called the court to order and Joyce was the first case on the morning docket. *The state vs Joyce Black, your Honor,* was the announcement. The Judge had Joyce stand and asked for her plea regarding the charges of 1) endangerment of a police officer, 2) being a co-conspirator in an unspecified number of local burglary cases and 3) resisting arrest. She pled not guilty, as the lawyer had suggested and he stood alongside her.   The Judge set her bail at $100,000, since there was no one to post her bail she was taken back to the jail cell in the station. There were gasps and lots of whispering when the Judge gave his ruling but even if she didn't have a criminal record her charges were quite serious. She turned and shuffled toward the door and back across the street to jail. She would have to wait for a trial to be set and that could easily be months away.

Once back to the jail cell, she stood motionless as the cuffs were removed from her wrists and ankles and she stepped into her new residence. It was not going to be a pleasant experience but she knew she could endure whatever came her way. She was a tough woman, having lost her fiancé in the war and never marrying. Her family was far from a demonstrative family when it came to emotions, such as expressing love and support. All of those years had hardened her exterior but she still had a tender heart and spending weeks and weeks, which became months and months in the jail cell, began to take a toll on her.

When questioned about all the stolen items, she tried to pass the blame to John Henry who was a known felon but her stories began to fall apart. No one had seen him riding a motorcycle into town on any of the nights of the reported break-ins and someone on a motorcycle couldn't transport all of those items. It was also true than no one remembered see Ballard's truck which was easily recognized in town on Saturday evenings and besides he seldom if ever went into town. His wife, Betty or daughter Joyce would do the shopping, so he didn't need to leave the farm except for trips to other towns.

She tried to make Junior an accomplice but most people couldn't image the gentle giant being involved in such heinous actions as stealing from others. But, since he was the youngest of the family members maybe his older brother exerted too much influence over him and made him do whatever he said! There was no doubt Junior had the strength to carry most of the household items which were taken. That lent some credibility to her story and raised some possibility to it being true.

Finger print experts at the various scenes had turned up the prints of Joyce and Junior but she was often in the houses doing cleaning and so finding her prints would be expected. Sometimes, Junior would go with her and wait while she finished her work and then they would head to the diner. There didn't seem to be anything suspicious about either of their prints being there but the lead detective began to think maybe there was more to their prints being at all of those scenes than she cleaned those particular houses.

What items were recovered were put in the entrance of the police station and the individuals or families who had items taken during a break in were invited to come and claim their stolen items. However, they must show proof that particular items belonged to them by having a receipt or having something with the serial numbers. Most didn't actually have that information and you must remember, quite a bit of the stolen goods had been taken to pawn shops in various other towns. The owners were pretty much out of luck but their insurance had covered some of the replacement costs.

Those items which could be identified were returned to the rightful owners and all of them were either customers of Joyce, next door neighbors to her customers or family members of her customers! A bit too much of a coincidence to satisfy the detective and prosecutor. Those items which remained unclaimed were auctioned off and some folks got their possessions back but ended up paying for them again.

After 6 months in the local jail, Joyce was about to offer some truth, if it meant leniency. She didn't want to spend years in prison because she saw what it did to John Henry and didn't want to be like him. So, when the detective approached her with a deal, she decided to take it. If she confessed to what actually happened her sentence would be commuted to time served and be on probation for 5 years.

She explained how she and Junior would gain access to the houses and take certain items, like flat screen television sets, laptop computers, answering machines, silverware and jewelry all of which were just usually setting around. They avoided taking too much of the jewelry at one time, so it wouldn't be noticed and the owners would simply think they had misplaced it. If there were any guns they would take all of them. Money was always a target but not too many had a lot of cash lying around but a few hundred here and there added up after a while.

She knew when the family would be gone so getting in was safe and easy since she had keys to a lot of the houses. For the ones that she didn't have keys it was easy to break a window and get in or to cut the wires on an alarm system if there was one but few homes in the city had them. With the alarm disabled the police would not be notified and they had all the time in the world to get what they wanted and load it in the van. They had it down to a science and had gotten away with it for quite a few years!

She admitted everyone in the family played a role, along with her and Junior. Her father sold the weapons at gun shows in other counties, John Henry could paint and restore the motorcycles, scooters and bicycles and her Mom would enjoy a new appliance or TV every few months. She also told of taking the items to pawn shops and pawning them. Since she didn't plan to go back for them, she didn't keep any of the pawn receipts. The shops were named and the police went to the shops to search for items she had taken there and left. If any of the items were able to be identified by serial numbers or by names engraved on them, the pawn shops lost the items and were warned about their license being suspended for selling stolen goods. None of the shop owners were arrested but it did create quite a stir in several of the surrounding towns.

Rex was able to identify his answering machine by the messages which had not been erased and the 4-wheeler was reclaimed. His guns couldn't be definitely identified so they were gone for good. His flat screen TV was in the house at the Black's farm so it was also returned because he had the receipt which included a serial number. The DVD player was gone but he had already replaced it. The tools from the basement had some identifying marks and most of them were returned. The Callahan's hadn't lost everything but the same could not be said for the Blacks!

When the details of the offered deal for Joyce was finalized, she was released and returned to the house. While she had been incarcerated the house sat empty and no one made any repairs. With no humans living there, it became the home for all kinds of critters from mice to squirrels, to birds, to bats, to insects and even a scroungy looking dog. It was obvious she couldn't live there, so her aunt Betty offered to let her live with them while the house was repaired. It took several months to get the house back into a livable condition but during that time, Joyce realized she was not really welcome in the community and didn't want to move back into the house because of all the memories. She decided to put the house and land up for sale. He plan was to take the money and go somewhere else to start a new life. In a new town no one would know her or her history and a fresh start was what she needed.

Ironically, Rex found a family, the Smiths who was really interested and brought a proposed contract to her. He let her know there was no hard feelings about what happened but he wished her well in getting a new start. She accepted the offer and within a few weeks, the deal was closed and she packed up her few belongings which were either in the house or at Betty's. She loaded her van and drove away, no one ever saw or heard of her again. She didn't even come back when Betty passed away about 5 years after Joyce had left town. Seeing her hometown in the rearview mirror was the best day she'd known in quite a few years!

Betty had enjoyed Joyce being there because she had been a big help in caring for Jeremiah. No matter what she had done, Betty considered her family and wouldn't turn her back on her. The community wasn't so forgiving and she was told to not come back to the church. She also couldn't find work because no one would hire her as a cleaning lady. None of the businesses were willing to hire her either. She actually had no income, so if it hadn't been for Betty, she would have really been in trouble. Selling some of the furnishings of the house did provide her with a few dollars but not enough to live on. It is quite true, crime doesn't pay!

Chapter 14

The Callahan's never regretted buying the Moore farm and making friends with the Jones, as well as Stan and his family. They were sorry the Blacks never came around to be good neighbors but the Smiths who bought the Black's property turned out to be great neighbors and good friends. After purchasing the property, the Smiths tore down the old house and replaced it with a beautiful two-story home. The old barn was gone and a separate standing 3-car garage was built in its place. The lane coming past the Jones' house was enlarged and turned into a very smooth drive due to the multiple loads of gravel which were hauled in.

In addition to the improvements, they not only would keep an eye on the Callahan's cabin on a regular basis but were quite helpful neighbors for the Jones. Hunting on each other's property was never a problem and besides Mr. Smith was the owner of a gun store in town and enjoyed hunting as well. They had moved from another town not too far away.

Jeremiah never fully recovered from the stroke but Betty was a tremendous caregiver. His sons did finally come to visit for a few days at the holidays but why they stayed away was never discussed. Whenever they came both Jeremiah and Betty were thrilled. The grandchildren were able to visit along with their parents and learned they had two amazing grandparents. During the summer when school was out, the older ones would come for a few weeks and it was a grand time of creating memories and letting the city-slicker kids learn about life outside of the city limits! They loved it and had great stories to tell their friends and classmates when the visit ended and they went back home to their parents and started school.

The break-ins had ended and life in the little town settled into a slow and predictable pace. Whenever the Callahan family could get away and go to the cabin, they headed out of town for a weekend or day of relaxation, even if it involved some work. You see, working at the cabin was not a chore, it was quite therapeutic and everyone would pitch in to do something. Keeping the grass cut was the major project and as fall drew near, getting ready to hunt meant planting fields with something for the deer to eat, putting out cameras and repositioning deer stands.

Tales of various hunts became traditions, especially as the men gathered and the younger members matured with some of them taking up the family tradition of hunting. The surest way to know if you are IN the family, is to listen to the stories being told and if you are NOT in them you are not actually in the family!

What are some of those stories? Well, what happens in the woods stays in the woods! If you really want to know you'll have to experience a hunting adventure for yourself and then maybe you'll know what I mean by *what happens in the woods, stays in the woods....*

Acknowledgements

My sincere thanks for the editing crew: Lee, Scott, Renee and Jason. Their discerning eyes and knowledge of creative writing helped to make this book a completed work!

Thank you to my brother, Dale who owns a farm outside of a small town in Kentucky. His real-life experiences are the foundation of the hunting stories but the fictional story is not based on actual people or incidents.

Not everyone has an interest in or a family history of hunting but there are solid reasons for hunting and reducing the number of deer. Venison is a healthy food, very lean with no fat and low in cholesterol. An over population of these beautiful creatures results in unhealthy animals due to a lack of adequate food and multiple incidents of vehicles hitting deer on the highways which often result in the death of the animals and sometimes to the drivers of those vehicles.

I hope you enjoyed the story....